Curiosity overcoming her caution, Dido approached the heap once more and pulled aside some folds of canvas. A sort of writhing motion went on in the middle of the heap, the sailcloth was displaced, and suddenly, rather as a serpent darts out of its hole, the figure of a tall, veiled lady uncoiled and shot from under the pile of stuff. She towered over the quailing Dido, who would have run for it had she not been held fast by the ear.

"What are you doing here?" the lady said in a low, grating tone.

"P-p-please, ma'am, I d-didn't mean no harm!" gulped Dido. "I was only looking for a c-c-corkscrew!"

"A likely story! Prying and meddling where you'd no business to be! Repulsive child! You deserve to be severely punished. Now, listen here, miss!"

"Y-y-yes, ma'am?"

"If you so much as mention that you have seen me to anyone—anyone at all—I shall learn of it. And it will be the worse for you. You wish to return to England, do you not?"

"Yes, ma'am," Dido whispered, very much astonished.

"Then you had better keep a still tongue in your head! Otherwise, your chances of ever seeing London River again are very, very small. Do you understand? Now—go!"

JOAN AIKEN, daughter of American writer Conrad Aiken, was born in Rye, Sussex, England. She is well known to young readers through her Laurel-Leaf editions of *The Wolves of Willoughby Chase* and *Black Hearts in Battersea*.

NIGHTBIRDS ON NANTUCKET

Joan Aiken

Published by
Dell Publishing Co., Inc.
1 Dag Hammarskjold Plaza
New York, New York 10017

Laurel-Leaf Library ® TM 766734,
Dell Publishing Co., Inc.

ISBN: 0-440-96370-2

RL: 6.0

Reprinted by arrangement with
Doubleday & Company, Inc.
Printed in the United States of America
First Laurel-Leaf printing—May 1981
Third Laurel-Leaf printing—October 1981

I am grateful to the whaling museums at Nantucket and New Bedford, from whom I obtained much valuable information, and to the latter for their instructive glossary of whaling terms.

CHAPTER ONE

On board the Sarah Casket. *The sleeper wakes. Tale of the pink whale. Half a world from home.*

LATE IN THE middle watch of a calm winter's night, many years ago, a square-rigged, three-masted ship, the *Sarah Casket*, was making her way slowly through northern seas under a blaze of stars. A bitter, teasing cold lurked in the air; frost glimmered on the ship's white decks and tinseled her shrouds; long icicles sometimes fell chiming from the spars to the planks beneath. No other sound could be heard in the silent night, save, from far away, the faint barking of seals.

On the deck a child lay sleeping in a wooden box filled with layers of straw. Sheepskins, covering her warmly, concealed her size, but from her face and tangled hair, her age might have been guessed at as seven or eight. Had it not been for her breath, ascending thread-like into the arctic air, she would have seemed more like a wax doll than a human being, so still and pale did she lie. Nearby squatted a boy, hunched up, his arms round his knees, gravely watching over her. It was his turn below, and by rights he should have been in his bunk, but whenever he had any time to spare he chose to spend it by the sleeping child.

She had been asleep for more than ten months.

Presently a bell rang and the watches changed. Bearded sailors came yawning on deck, others went below; one, as he passed the boy, called out, "Hey, there, Nate! No sign of life yet, then?"

The boy shook his head without replying.

One or two of the men said, "Why don't you give over, boy? She'll never wake in this world."

And one, a narrow-faced character with close-set eyes and a crafty, foxy look to him, said sourly, "Why waste your time, you young fool? If it weren't for you and our sainted captain she'd have been food for the barracootas long ago."

"Nay, don't say that, Mr. Slighcarp," somebody protested. "She've brought us greasy luck so far, hain't she? We're nigh as full with whale oil as we can hold."

"Hah!" sneered the man called Slighcarp. "What's *she* to do with the luck? We'd have had it whether we picked her up or no. I say she'd be best overboard before it changes. I've allus hated serving on a chick frigate."

He went below, muttering angrily. Meanwhile the boy, Nate, calmly, and taking no notice of these remarks, addressed himself to the sleeping child.

"Come on now, young 'un," he said. "It's your suppertime."

One or two of the men lingered to watch him as he carefully raised the child with one arm and then, tilting a tin coffeepot which he held in the other hand, poured down her throat a thick, black mixture of whale oil and molasses. She swallowed it in her sleep. Her eyelids never even fluttered. When the pot was empty, Nate laid her down again in her straw nest and replaced the sheepskins.

"Blest if *I'd* care to live on such stuff," one of the men muttered. "Still and all, I guess you've kept her alive with it, Nate, eh? She'd have been skinny enough by now, but for you."

"Guess I like looking after live creatures," Nate said mildly. "I'd been a-wanting summat to care for ever since my bird, Mr. Jenkins, flew away in the streets of New Bedford just before we sailed. And Cap'n Casket says there's no more nourishing food in this world than whale oil and m'lasses. Ye can see the young 'un thrives on it, anyways; six inches she've grown since I had the feeding of her."

"And for what?" snarled the first mate, the foxy Mr. Slighcarp, reappearing from the afterhatchway. "What pleasure is it for us to see our vittles vanishing down that brat's throat when, so far as anyone can see, it's all for Habakkuk? Break it up, now, men! Those that's going below, *get* below!"

The men were dispersing quickly, when a cry from aloft galvanized them in a different way.

"Blo-o-ows! Thar she *blows!*"

The lookout in the crosstrees was dancing up and down, dislodging, in his excitement, about a hundred-weight of icicles, which came clanking and tinkling to the deck. His arm was extended straight forward.

"Whale-o! Dead ahead, not more'n a mile!"

And indeed, on the horizon a pale, silvery spout of water could just be seen.

Like ants the men scurried about the ship while Mr. Slighcarp shouted orders.

"Set royals and t'gallants! Bend on stuns'ls! Lower the boats!"

Light as leaves, three long cedarwood whaleboats glided down from the davits onto the calm sea. But just before the boats were manned a startling thing occurred. As if roused by all the commotion, the child, lying in her straw-filled box, turned, stretched, and yawned, drawing thin hands from under the sheepskin to knuckle her still-shut eyes. The boy Nate had gone below, but one of the sailors running by noticed her and exclaimed, "Land sakes to glory! Look at the supercargo! She's stirring! She's waking!"

"Devil's teeth, man! Never mind the scrawny brat now! See to the boats!" bellowed Mr. Slighcarp.

Thus urged, the men swung nimbly to their places in the boats, but they went with many a backward look at the child, who was moving restlessly now, under the pile of sheepskins, still with her eyes tight shut. Waves of color passed over her pale face.

But the boats had sped away, hissing in white parallels over the dark sea before the child finally opened her eyes and struggled to a sitting position.

She looked about her blankly. All was still now on board the whaler. Only a few shipkeepers remained, and they were occupied elsewhere.

The child stared vaguely about her until at length her eyes began to fix, with puzzled intelligence, on the few things visible in the dim light from a lantern hanging over her head. She could see white-frosted planking, a massive tangle of rigging between her and the stars, a dark bulk, the tryworks amidships, and, above, the gleam of spare tools lodged on the skids.

"This ain't the *Dark Dew*," she murmured, half to herself. "Where can I be?"

The boy, Nate, was passing at that moment. When he heard her voice he started, nearly dropping the mug he carried. Then he turned and cautiously approached her.

"Well, I'll be gallied!" he breathed in amazement. "If it isn't the Sleeping Beauty woke up at last!"

The child stared at him wonderingly, and he stared back at her. He saw a girl with a pointed face and long, tangled brown hair hanging over her shoulders. She looked older now she was awake—perhaps nine or ten, he guessed. She saw a thin boy of about sixteen, hollow-cheeked and with eyes set so deep that it was impossible to guess their color.

"*You* aren't Simon," she said wonderingly. "Where's Simon?"

"Human language, too! Who's Simon?"

"My friend."

"There's no Simon on board this hooker," the boy said, squatting down beside her. "Here, want a mug o' chowder? It's hot. I was just taking it to the steersman—he's my uncle 'Lige. But you might as well have it."

"Thank you," she said. She seemed dreamy, still only half-awake, but the hot soup roused her. "What's your name?" she asked.

"Nathaniel Pardon. 'Nate,' they call me. What's yours?"

"Dido Twite."

"Dido—that's a funny name. I've heard of 'Dionis'—never 'Dido.' You're a Britisher, ain't you?"

"O' course I am," she said, puzzled. "Ain't you?"

"Not me. I'm a Nantucketer." And he sang softly:

*   *   *

"Oh, blue blows the lilac and green grows the corn,
And the isle of Nantucket is where I was born,
Sweet isle of Nantucket! where the plums are so
    red,
Ten hours and twelve minutes southeast of Gay
    Head."

"Never heard of it," Dido said. "What ship's this, then?"

"The *Sarah Casket,* out of Nantucket."

"Did you pick me up?" she asked, knitting her brows together painfully in an effort to recall what had happened.

"Sure, we picked you up in the North Sea, floating like a bit o' brit. And from that day to this you've lain on the deck snoring louder'n a grampus; *I* never thought you'd trouble to wake up. You seemed all set to sleep till Judgment. Cap'n Casket allowed as how you musta had a bang on the head, maybe from a floating spar, to knock you into such an everlasting snooze. Can you remember what happened to you?"

"Our ship, the *Dark Dew,* caught fire," she murmured, rubbing her forehead. "Me and Simon was in the sea, hanging onto the mast. Simon was my friend—he was on this ship, bound for Hanover, and I stowed away too, for a lark, so's to be with him. . . . You're sure you didn't pick up a boy called Simon?"

"No, honey," he said gently. "But there's plenty shipping off the British coast where we found you. Maybe someone else took him on board."

"Yes, reckon that's so," Dido agreed eagerly. "He'll be all right, won't he? I wouldn't like no harm to come to Simon, acos he was the only person who was ever kind to me. He was the lodger at my ma's house. He used to tell me stories and took me to the fair. Soon's we get home I'll ask if he's safe. When do we get to port?"

" 'Bout eight months from now. Maybe nine."

"Eight *months*? Are you crazy? Hey, where in Jonah's name are we?"

"North o' Cape East—in the Arctic Ocean." Plainly this meant nothing to Dido, so he explained, "Soon's our casks are all full we'll be heading down across the Pacific and round Cape Horn, back to Nantucket. That'll set you a step on your way. Guess you can find some packet out o' New Bedford or Boston that'll take you to England. You'll be home in under a year."

"Not before?"

"Well," Nate said, "we've had you on board ten months. You've traveled a long way since we picked you up."

Dido looked quite dazed at this information. "How *did* you come to pick me up?" she asked presently.

For the first time Nate appeared slightly embarrassed. "Well," he explained hesitantly, "we was a mite off course. It was this how, you see. Cap'n had fixed to go after sperm whales in the western grounds, so we was a-cruisin' off Madeira. And then the Old Man—he's a fine captain, just old pie on knowing where they're running, could raise you a whale in a plate o' sand, but he's funny in one way, awful peculiar—"

He stopped, his mouth open.

"Go on," said Dido. "How's he funny?"

A voice from behind made her start.

"What is thee doing up on deck, Nate?" it said sternly. "Thee should be in thy bunk at this hour."

Dido turned and saw a tall man, dressed all in black. He had a long black beard almost covering his white shirtfront; his face was severe, but two great mournful eyes in it seemed as if they paid little attention to the words he spoke; they were fixed elsewhere, on vacancy.

"I—I'm sorry, sir, Cap'n Casket," Nate said, stammering a little. "I was taking a hot drink to Uncle 'Lije when I saw the little girl had wakened up."

"So she has. So she has. How strange," murmured Captain Casket, bending his eyes on Dido for the first time. "Does thee feel better for thy long sleep, my dear?"

"Yes, thank you, mister," Dido answered bashfully.

"Nate, since the little one has woken, thee had better fetch her some slops."

"Yes, sir, Cap'n. Shall I fetch some o' Miss Du—"

"Don't be a fool, boy!" Captain Casket said sharply. "Thee knows it is impossible. They—they would be too small. There must be some boys' gear in one of the slop chests. Fetch out a bundle. And shears: that long hair won't do aboard a whaler."

"Yes, sir." Nate ran off in a hurry. Captain Casket fixed his sad, wandering eyes on Dido, but they soon moved back to the horizon and, heaving a deep sigh, he seemed to forget her. She was in too much awe of him to speak.

At length, turning to her again, he said, "Has thee family and friends in England, my child?"

"Y-yes, sir!"

"Poor souls. This will have been a sorrowful time

for them. No matter, the joy when thee is restored to them will be all the greater."

"Yes, sir. Thank you for picking me up," Dido said bravely.

"Providence must have ordered that we should be sailing by. His ways are strange." Captain Casket's grave face lightened in a smile of rare sweetness and simplicity; he added, "Now thee has wakened up, my child, thee can be of considerable help to me in thy turn."

"Yes, sir. H-how?"

"Tomorrow will be soon enough to explain the task I have in mind for thee. I will not burden thee tonight. Here comes Nate now with the clothes. When thee has put them on, thee had better sleep again."

He moved away silently over the deck.

Nate came running with an armful of clothes and a great pair of shears. He proceeded to chop off most of Dido's hair.

"That feels better," she said, shaking her head. "Can't think how it come to be so long, it never used. It musta growed while I was sleeping. Why won't long hair do aboard a whaler?"

"Why? Because o' the gurry," Nate said, grinning. "Now, can you fix yourself up in them things?"

"What's gurry?"

"Slime. You'll see at cutting-in time, if the men have had greasy luck."

Nate had brought a boy's nankeen breeches and shirt, a monkey jacket, red drawers, Falmouth stockings, and a pair of leather brogans.

"These'll be too big for me," Dido said. But she soon found they were not. "Great snakes! I musta growed six inches since I been a-laying here. I'm as big as a 'leven-year-old."

"Guess that'll be all the whale oil. We could see it was doin' you good. You used to cough considerable at first, but you haven't done so for months."

Dido looked around to make sure they were not overheard. "What were you going to tell me about Captain Casket? And why does he talk in that queer way?"

"He's a Friend—a Quaker—that's why. And what I was going to tell you—" Nate in his turn glanced behind him and, seeing the deck was clear, went on: "He's allus had a kind of an uncommon fancy, you see—ever since he was a boy, Uncle 'Lije says. First off, on this trip it warn't so noticeable. His old lady, Mrs. Casket, she sailed along with us because she warn't well and they reckoned sea air would do good. But it didn't. She took sick and died, poor soul, afore we ever sighted Santa Cruz. When she was on board he kept to plain whaling. But when she died and—" Nate came to a halt and started again. "She was a mite solemnlike and fussy in her ways, and scared to death of the sea, but there warn't no real harm in her. She used to make gingerbread and molasses cookies sometimes, afore she was took ill. Can you bake cookies?" he asked Dido.

"No."

"Oh. Well, after she died Cap'n Casket got quieter and quieter. Never smiled (not that he was ever much of a one for a joke), never spoke. One day he said he saw the pink whale."

"What's queer about that?" asked the ignorant Dido.

"What's queer? Well, they don't *come* pink whales,

that's all! But Uncle 'Lije—he's second mate on this here craft—says Cap'n Casket forever had this notion that one day he *would* see one—on account of summat as happened when he was a boy. Some folks think he's a bit touched about it, though other ways he's sensible enough. Well, one day off Madeira he swore he'd seen a pink whale and nothing would do but we must chase it. Why? Uncle 'Lije asks. Cap'n Casket says he wants to get close enough to take a good look at it. Seems there's summat special about it he's keen to find out. What? Don't ask me. No, he don't want to *catch* it, just study it. Then Mr. Slighcarp—he's the first mate—he allowed as we'd better humor the Old Man, so he let on as he'd seen it too. We clapped on sail and went chasing up past Finisterre and Ushant and Land's End, and next thing we was squeezing through the North Sea past London River. Clean lost the pink whale, but that's where we picked *you* up. Only you was fast asleep and wouldn't wake to tell us where your home port was. For all we knew, you mighta been a Feejee Islander. So I adopted you, kind of like a mascot because I'd lost my pet myna bird. Then Cap'n Casket, he sees the pink whale again, off John O' Groat's, and she leads us a fair dance right round the Horn and up past the Galapagos and Alaska to where we are now."

"Did you ever catch her?"

"Not likely! No one's ever seed her but Mr. Slighcarp and the Old Man. Still, we had good luck, we caught plenty other whales after that first little dummy run. But some o' the men was a bit ashamed of getting so far off the whaling grounds as we was when we picked you up."

Suddenly Dido's lip quivered.

"I wish you hadn't! I wish some English ship had picked me up!"

"Well, there's ingratitude!" Nate said indignantly. He added in a gentler tone, "We couldn't leave you to drown, now, could we? You'll get home soon enough."

But, for Dido, the dreamlike strangeness of her surroundings, the huge, dark, frosted ship, the blazing arctic sky across which mysterious arches and curtains and streamers of red and green now flickered—most of all, the fact, only half-understood, that she was an immense distance, half a world away from home—all this was suddenly too much to be borne. She flung herself down on the pile of sheepskins and cried as if her heart would break.

"There, there!" said Nate uncomfortably. "Come now, don't take on so, don't! Supposin' somebody was to see you?"

"I don't care!" wept Dido. "I wish I was at home. Oh, I wish I was at home *now!*"

Finding her inconsolable, Nate did the kindest thing; he helped her back into her straw bed, covered her warmly with sheepskins again, and left her, giving her a cautious pat on the shoulder.

"Cheer up!" he whispered. "Things'll look better in the morning. They allus does."

But Dido was not listening to him. Curled up like a dormouse, she burrowed deeper under the sheepskins, hid her face in the prickly straw, and cried herself to sleep.

CHAPTER TWO

*The captured whale. The mysterious weeper. Captain
Casket's task.*

WHEN DIDO WOKE once more dawn had broken, wild
and red and dim. The ice-covered ship gleamed like a
Christmas tree. What had roused her were the shouts
of the men, who had returned towing a large sperm
whale, their three boats spread around it like tugs.
Dido was astonished at the sight of this huge, mouse-
colored monster, almost as big as the ship, it seemed,
with its steep face, flat and featureless as the side of a
house. At first, in alarm, thinking it was still alive,
she scrambled out of her straw bed and retreated to
the far side of the deck. But then she realized that it
was dead and the men were making it fast to the ship.

"What are they going to do with it?" she asked
Nate, who ran along the deck with five mugs of hot
coffee clutched precariously in each hand. By day he
was revealed as a long, lanky redhead, with friendly,
gray eyes and a great many freckles.

"Cut-in, o' course. I can't stop now, chick. Why

don't you step down to the camboose and get some breakfast?"

Dido guessed that the camboose must be the kitchen, but she was too interested in what the men were doing to leave the deck for a while.

They had the whale's body slung on ropes from the rigging, and now, by winding a massive windlass, were causing it to turn over and over in the sea. Meanwhile they sang:

> *"Oh, whaling is my only failing*
> *Sailing whaling's done for me!*
> *Life's all Bible leaves and bailing.*
> *Never ask me in when there's decent folk to tea!"*

At the same time several men were skillfully slicing with sharp, spadelike tools so that the blubber, or skin, was peeled off the whale's body in a spiral, like orange peel. Sections of this blubber strip were removed and lowered through a forward hatchway.

> *"Hush your weeping and your wailing,*
> *Six-and-thirty months I'll be at sea—*
> *Tears and grumbles are unavailing.*
> *And never ask me in when there's decent folk to tea!"*

"What do they do with it down there?" Dido asked a passing man. He scowled at her. It was Mr. Slighcarp, the first mate.

"Ho! *You've* woken up to plague us, have you? Don't you go near the tryworks or I'll spank you with a deck spade."

"They mince it up in the blubber room, ready to be boiled down for oil," another, more good-natured man told her. "Mr. Pardon, the second mate, 'll show you sometime. He's right pleased to hear you've woken up at last."

"Which is the tryworks, mister?"

"Over there."

She looked where he pointed and saw a brick furnace in the middle of the deck, with huge metal pots built in above. Men were feeding the fire in the furnace with bits of tarred rope and frizzled scraps of whale, while others tossed chunks of blubber into the pots. Soon the brew in them began to melt and bubble. Thick, black, greasy smoke rolled over the deck.

"Cor, love a lily-white *duck!*" gasped Dido as a murky bank of the smoke surged towards her and almost smothered her. "I never in all my born smelt such a smell, *never!* It's enough to make a bad egg bust out crying and go home to mother."

Nate, who was passing with the empty mugs, laughed. "You'd better get used to it," he said. "There's going to be plenty more afore we're through."

The men worked like furies all through the morning in order to get as much as possible done while the brief daylight lasted. At noon a little old bowlegged Negro, whom everybody addressed affectionately as "Doctor," came on deck with a steaming cauldron of something that smelled very appetizing, and the men helped themselves from it when they could snatch a moment from their labors.

"Go and help yourself!" Nate called to Dido—he was sharpening tools on a grindstone.

Rather timidly she approached the cook, who gave

her a flashing white grin and handed her a tin panni-
kin of hash.

"You like lobscouse, eh? Best lobscouse from here
to Christmas Island, eh Mr. Pardon? Make a change
from whale oil, I b'lieve?"

Mr. Pardon, the white-haired, kindly-faced second
mate, smiled at Dido and said:

"Bless me! Who'd 'a taken you for the poor little
shriveled poke we hauled on board ten months ago?"

"What's lobscouse made of?" Dido asked, looking
suspiciously at the mixture in her pan. "Why, corned
beef and hardtack and good salt water. Eat it up! You
can still do wi' a bit more flesh on your bones."

By this time the whole deck was covered with an
unbelievable mess of oil and slime and bits of the
whale's thin outer skin. The sails were blackened by
smoke, and the rigging was all furred up with greasy
soot.

"This is a mucky trade, ennit?" Dido said to Nate,
who was still whirling away at his grindstone, sharpening the cutting spades as they became blunted by
use. "What do they want the whale oil for, anyways?"

"Oh, lamps and horses' legs," he answered vaguely.
"And trains, I guess. Here, pass this down to Uncle
'Lije as you're about, won't you? Mind the slumgul-
lion."

> "When I'm old and weak and ailing
> Sailing whaling still I'll be;
> Lash me standing to the lash railing
> And never speak my name when there's decent folk
>   to tea."

came the voices from the windlass.

Dido moved cautiously over the littered deck, but she had the ill-fortune to tread on a particularly slippery patch of oil, lost her footing, and slid, entangling the cutting spade she carried with the legs of Mr. Slighcarp as he stretched up to pull down a blanket of blubber from the hook. He fell sprawling, with the blubber on top of him, and, when he rose, cursed Dido most evilly. Matters were not helped by the shouts of laughter from the crew.

"I—I'm sorry, mister," Dido gulped, trying to suppress her own giggles. "I couldn't help it, honest!"

"Git below!" snarled Mr. Slighcarp. "I'll have no frogspawn like you littering the deck while I'm in charge. Git, or I'll toss you overboard!"

Terrified at this threat, Dido picked herself up and scurried away. Guided by a gesture and a wink from Nate, she slipped down a hatchway and found herself suddenly out of the noise and stink and bustle, on a neat little winding stair, white-painted and silent. Where did it lead? On she went, cautiously exploring, and presently entered a good-sized stateroom, also white-painted, and very tidy. A rocking chair stood by a glowing stove; a swinging bed was made up with a patchwork quilt; over this hung a compass, upside down. Dido studied the compass for a moment, but it meant nothing to her; nor did the charts spread on the table. A huge book held them down; she opened it; it was the Bible. While sniffing the petals of a blooming pink geranium on a shelf, she was startled by a small sound from somewhere close at hand. It sounded like a sob.

Arrested, Dido stood motionless, listening. Yes! There again! More sobs, half-stifled at first, then breaking into a low, wailing cry: *"Mamma! Oh, Mamma!"*

Dido thought she had never in her life heard a sound so lonely and desolate.

The cabin was empty; where, then, did the voice come from? There were two doors, one on each side, in the white paneling. Trying them, she found that both were locked, but the sound seemed to come from behind the right-hand one. When she tried it a frightened voice whispered, "Who's there?"

"It's me. Dido Twite. Who are you?"

No reply. Dead silence from beyond the door. Dido tried again.

"Come on! Do say summat! I ain't a-going to bite you! Why are you shut in?"

No answer.

"Croopus," Dido sighed to herself. "This is a rum brig and no mistake. Pink whales and spooky voices. Don't I jist wish I was safe home."

A whisper hit her ear like a small cold draught. She leaned to catch what it said.

"I believe you're Aunt Tribulation. *Go away!*"

"I'm Dido Twite, I tell you!"

"Go away!"

"Pooh," said Dido, hurt. "All right, I jist will. And you can holler for me next time." She made her way back on deck, greatly puzzled. Whose could the voice be? No one she had seen or heard of yet, that was certain. It had sounded like a child—but nobody had mentioned a child.

This time, keeping well clear of the tryworks and the fierce Mr. Slighcarp, she made her way to the quarterdeck. There she found Captain Casket, silent, withdrawn, and stern-looking. He had his back to her and was studying the compass in the binnacle, so she tiptoed to the rail and stood watching two gulls on an ice floe as they quarreled over a scrap of blubber.

Presently she felt a chilly sensation in her shoulder blades and turned to find that Captain Casket had his strange, sad eyes fixed on her.

He cleared his throat once or twice, as if speaking were not a very common activity with him, and said, "What is thy name, child?"

"D-Dido, sir. Dido Twite."

"A heathen name," the captain murmured. "No matter. There may be godliness within." He scrutinized her with an intent, close regard, as if measuring her for some purpose he had in mind. Dido looked back wonderingly.

At last he said, "Thee has a firm chin, my child, and a philanthropic brow."

"Has—have I?" Dido said, surprised. "Coo, I never knew. Maybe I got some o' the gurry on it when I fell down." She rubbed her forehead with her sleeve.

"I need thy help," Captain Casket went on. "Thee looks like a strong, brave character."

Am I? Dido wondered. She realized with surprise that she did feel strong, far stronger than she had been before she fell into her ten-month sleep.

"Does thee think thee can be kind but firm with somebody not so blessed in courage and strength?"

Suddenly Dido began to guess what he was leading up to. Forgetting her awe of him, she blurted out, "Well, mister, if it's anything to do with that poor little thing that's locked up downstairs, I can tell you straight I think it's a wicked shame. How would *you* like to be locked up?"

Captain Casket looked at her sadly. "Child, thee

doesn't understand," he said. "I am not her jailer. She did it herself. She bolted herself in when her mamma died. No words of mine avail to draw her forth."

"Ohhhh!" Dido breathed, round-eyed. "Mercy gracious, why ever'd she do that? Is she your little girl, then?"

"Yes," he said, sighing.

"What's her name? How old is she?" Dido was all curiosity. What a queer thing, to shut oneself in a cabin!

"She's nine," he said heavily. "Her name is Dutiful Penitence Casket."

"Croopus," Dido murmured.

"Her mamma, my dear wife, though endowed with every Christian virtue, had one foolish failing," he went on, half to himself. "This was her incurable fear of the sea. I thought that if I took her with me on a voyage it would allay her fear and improve her delicate health. Fool! Fool that I was. From the very night she came on board she closed the curtains tight across the portholes of the cabin and never so much as glanced out. Nor never set foot out on deck, neither she nor the child. Nor never let any of the crew come near the cabin." He paused and added in a lower tone, "But the ways of Providence are strange to us."

"And so the poor lady took and died?" Dido said compassionately, as he seemed to have come to a stop.

"Yes, my child. And Penitence, who had imbibed her mother's fears, believed the sea had caused her death."

"So she shut herself up."

"From that day to this," he agreed, sighing. "I believe she thinks the sea will kill her too, if she ventures out."

"Coo," said Dido. "What a jobberknoll. But what does she do for prog—for vittles?"

"The little cabin where she slept next to my wife is also the store where my dear Sarah kept preserves and spices and medicines. I believe Penitence has been living on beach-plum jelly and sassafras all this time."

"Well, my ma would soon clobber me if I went on in such a way," said Dido frankly. "And if you was to ask me, *I* think she sounds touched in the upper works. But I can see what you wants. You wants me to put the wheedle on her and make her come out, ain't that so?"

"Yes, my child. Thee has guessed right. I have a hatred of violence or trickery; I would not force her to come out. But if thee can somehow *persuade* her . . ." He looked at Dido hopefully and added, "After all, we did pull thee out of the sea. We saved thy life."

Ignoring this, Dido looked at him sharply and asked, "Why didn't you get Nate or Mr. Pardon to have a go with the little girl?"

Captain Casket appeared slightly embarrassed. At last he said, "My child, I tell thee this in confidence. The crew are not aware that Penitence has locked herself up in this way. They—they believe that she is ailing. To have it known that she defies me would be bad for discipline. Thee"—he gazed at her anxiously —"thee will not divulge what I have told thee, my dear?"

"Oh, *now* I twig your lay," Dido said. He looked bewildered. "I see why you been so havey-cavey about her. All right, I'll keep mum. And I don't mind having a try."

"Thee is a good child. I am truly grateful," Captain Casket said almost humbly. "I feel thee may succeed where I have failed."

Dido gave him a shrewd look. "If I manage to wheedle her out, will you see I gets a passage on the fust ship that'll take me back to England?"

"Anything in my power I shall do," he assured her quickly. "As soon as we return to New Bedford I shall inquire about sailings."

"What'll happen to Dutiful Penitence then?"

"Oh, my sister Tribulation will look after her," Captain Casket said, avoiding her eyes. "Now I must leave thee to oversee the cutting-in. Goodby, my child. Thee may have the use of my stateroom. I will move into Mr. Slighcarp's cabin."

As he walked aft, rather fast, Dido stared after him thoughtfully. Why had he been so anxious to get away? Somehow she felt that, although he seemed a good man, she could not entirely trust Captain Casket. And what a ninny to let his daughter get the upper hand in so decided a way! He's weak, Dido decided. Means well, but he's weak. That's the sort that allus lets you down in the end.

Still, she thought, I can look after meself. I'm a big girl now. And she surveyed her extra six inches with pride before squatting down, chin on fists, to consider the problem of how Dutiful Penitence Casket was to be persuaded out of her shell.

CHAPTER THREE

*Talking to Penitence. The veiled lady. Hopscotch.
Dido makes a promise.*

LONG AFTER DARK had fallen Dido was still loitering
on the quarterdeck, her brow wrinkled in thought.
Twice since her talk with Captain Casket she had
gone below, tapped on the panel in the captain's
stateroom, and tried to persuade the hidden occupant
of the little room beyond to come out. Her first at-
tempt had met with no response; next time, the only
reaction had been a fierce, miserable whisper from behind the panel: "Go away. Go *away*! Whoever you
are, I shan't come out. I know you're only trying to
trick me to go up on deck and be drowned!"

Dido saw that she would have to be clever.

"What do you do all day long in there?" she asked,
the beginnings of a plan sprouting in her mind.
There was no answer. She had not really expected
one. She went on, half to herself, "Well, I don't wonder you gets blue-deviled if you does nothing but sit
and think o' drowning all the time. Cheesy, *I* calls
it!"

She left the cabin, shutting the door behind her with a loud, annoying slam.

After more than sixteen hours of frantic, continuous work, the captured whale was all cut up and melted down; Mr. Slighcarp's watch staggered below, blind and speechless with fatigue. At last the moment arrived that Dido had been waiting for. She stretched, rose, left the quarterdeck, and went along to the try-works, which were simmering down, now, to a dull red glow. Half a dozen weary men were scrubbing the deck with ashes; their shadows flitted to and fro under a towering, arctic moon. From time to time they paused in their labors, dipped bits of hardtack in the still-molten blubber, and chewed them. The good-natured Mr. Pardon was supervising the work.

"Why, dearie," he said in surprise, "you shoulda been in your bunk hours agone. Cap'n Casket tells me he's given you his stateroom for to be company for little Miss Penitence. Mr. Slighcarp's not best pleased at having to move in with me, but 'tis more fitting for you than lying up here on a donkey's breakfast. And I guess you'll be better able than a man to look after that poor little ailing lass."

Dido nodded soberly. "Mr. Pardon," she said.

"Well, dearie?"

"What's Captain Casket's little girl like?"

"Like?" Mr. Pardon scratched his white head, puzzled. "Why, I guess she's like all little gals. Sews her sampler, reads her lesson—Mrs. Casket allus used to hear her lessons when she was alive, poor lady."

"But what's she like?" Dido persisted. "What kind o' games does she like to play?"

"Play? Why, I dunno as how she plays any *games*.

But my nephew Nate here'd know better'n I do; his home's right near to the Casket place."

"Games?" said Nate when appealed to. "Don't reckon she ever played any. Very quiet little thing, sorta peaky. Her ma allus kept her pretty much at her stitching and so forth.

"Blimey," muttered Dido, "What a setout. No wonder she's such a misery. Mr. Pardon, d'you reckon as how you could make me a shuttlecock for her? Out o' whalebone or summat? I could stick it with gulls' feathers."

"I don't see why not," Mr. Pardon said doubtfully. "Guess it would be simple enough. But what would Cap'n Casket think? Mrs. Casket allus used to say that toys were inventions of the Devil."

"I guess he'd have to put up with it," Dido said. "He asked me if I'd try to take Dutiful Penitence out o' herself. She's pining for her ma."

Nate was interested in the scheme. "I could make a whalebone bat," he offered. "And some checkers or spilikins."

"Could you? That'd be bang-up!"

Dido went below, well pleased with the way matters were shaping.

The big cabin was lit by a hanging whale-oil lamp. Dido turned the wick up to its brightest. Then she listened. No sound came from Dutiful Penitence, so Dido banged the cabin door, opened and shut some drawers several times as loudly as she could, and overturned a chair with a tremendous clatter.

She heard a sleepy stir from beyond the panel. "Papa, what's the matter?" said a scared voice. "Is it a storm?"

Dido made no answer. She climbed up onto the

chart table and then, after carefully judging the distance, jumped four feet to a wall shelf, where she clung like a squirrel. From there, making use of the hanging compass, she swung to the bed, landing with a thud. Then she crawled to the bedfoot, put her knee on an open drawer, and clawed herself across to another shelf, aware as she did so, though without showing it, that the panel had opened a crack and that she was being watched. She balanced on the shelf, gauging the distance to a chair.

"Who are you?" asked an astonished voice. "And what *do* you think you're doing? Where is Papa?"

"I told you already," Dido said without looking round. "I'm Dido Twite. Your pa's given me his cabin." She steadied herself and sprang. The chair fell, and threw her to the floor. "Drat it," Dido said coldly, getting up and rubbing her knee. "Now I shall have to start again."

"Start *what* again?"

Taking no notice of the question, Dido climbed back onto the chart table. This time she chose a different route, throwing herself like a flying fox onto a large sea chest, which seemed full of bottles, to judge from the loud clatter when she landed on it.

She scowled in concentration, considering a sideways clamber across the door as against an awkward diagonal jump to the bed. She chose the former.

"What are you doing?" the voice repeated.

Dido dragged herself up with difficulty and turned round. She was now perching like a gargoyle on a sort of dresser. "Why!" she said exasperatedly. "What d'you think I'm doing? What does it *look* as if I'm doing? Making cheese? I'm getting round the room without touching the floor, o' course, I shoulda thought any ninny coulda seen *that*. You must be a slowtop. Now, don't interrupt again. You put me off." She knit her brows and pressed her lips together, then with a mighty spring succeeded in launching herself from the dresser to the fallen chair, which slid conveniently across to the bed.

"Now I'm going to sleep," Dido announced. "Mind you don't make a noise and wake me." She turned out the light. All this time she had never looked towards the open hatchway. Yawning loudly, she snuggled down under the blankets. Silence fell.

After a longish pause the voice asked, "Why didn't you want to touch the floor?"

Dido made no answer, but, instead, let out a slight snore.

Very early next morning Dido, who needed little sleep after her ten-month nap, woke and scurried up on deck before any sound came from Dutiful Penitence.

The *Sarah Casket*, all her barrels now filled with whale oil, was speeding south under a clear sky. Some of the men were hard at work hammering in the lids of the great hogsheads, twice the height of Dido, before these were lowered into the hold; others were scrubbing every inch of the deck and bulwarks with ashes and bits of blubber, even climbing into the rigging to wipe the shrouds. Soot and ashes flew away on the fresh breeze, and the ship by degrees began to look so tidy and clean that Dido could hardly believe it was the same in which, only the day before, whale oil had run like greasy, dark ink over the deck.

The kindly Mr. Pardon had contrived time out of his duties to make a shuttlecock. He gave it to Dido. "It ain't very grand; I made a bit of a mux of it," he

apologized, "but I reckoned you'd druther have it
soon than *fancy*. I'll make a better one now I got the
hang—I'm real pleased to do it. Young 'uns should
have playthings. And Nate, he's fixing ye a right
handsome battledore, but 'twon't be finished yet a
piece, because Mr. Slighcarp's sent him up to scrub
the crow's-nest."

Dido looked up and saw a tiny figure—miles up, it
seemed—in the clear, piercing air. Nate waved a
scrubbing brush cheerfully, and she waved back.

"This here's a fust-rate shuttlecock," she told Mr.
Pardon. "Jist what I wanted. Cap'n Casket's little girl
will be astonished, I reckon."

"Don't forget your breakfast, dearie," Mr. Pardon
said as she turned to go below.

"That's a notion," Dido said. She added to herself,
"I dessay Dutiful Pen has had enough o' plum jelly
to last a lifetime; let's see what a sight o' summat else
does for her." She skipped along to the camboose by
the wheelhouse. "What's for breakfast?" she asked
briskly.

"Ah! Is little chick passenger!" The black cook
gave her his beaming grin. "I have nice fu-fu, also
nice plum duff; we celebrate last barrelful, see?"

"What's fu-fu?"

"Mush with molasses. Is varry good."

"No, thanks," Dido said, eying the black stuff dis-
tastefully. "Can I have two helps o' plum duff? I'll
take some down for Dutiful P. She might fancy it."

"Is picky and choosy, that one," the cook said,
shaking his head. "Is not fancy, my cooking." However he dealt out two large portions of delicious
raisin pudding, made with dripping and potash.

"You like some coffee?"

"Thanks, mister. Any milk?"

"Not yet, honey. Goat she took and died. In some month we make Galapagos Island. Then maybe coconut milk."

Dido ran down the companionway with the food. Back in the cabin she limbered up before breakfast by doing two circuits of the room, falling only once. While so engaged, she noticed that the panel had opened an inch, and that an eye was peering at her through the crack.

Refreshed, Dido sat down at the chart table, where she had put the plates of plum duff, and began to eat one portion with smacking sounds of enjoyment.

"Nibblish good prof," she remarked loudly. "Better'n my ma makes, anyhows."

When she had finished her plateful she got up, leaving the second portion untouched and well in view, took the shuttlecock out of her pocket and began to kick it into the air. As Mr. Pardon had said, it was not a very well-made one, being slightly unbalanced, and at first Dido found difficulty in keeping it up for more than two or three kicks. She persevered, however, bounding about the room until she was breathless and bruised from collisions with the furniture. Meanwhile she was watched with silent, astonished attention from the hatchway.

"This room ain't big enough," Dido complained presently, when she was becoming more experienced with the shuttlecock and had worked her score up to twenty-three. "I'm a-going on deck, I am, where there's plenty of room."

She departed, slamming the door behind her. Although strongly tempted to linger and look through the keyhole, she knew this would be foolish. Instead, she clattered up the companion stair and went out to the quarterdeck.

However, she soon found that there was little room, even here, to practice her game, for the men were tidying out the hold, to make room for the last casks of whale oil, and had brought all the stores up on deck. There was such a general hubbub of to-and-fro activity that Dido seemed to be constantly underfoot and in everybody's way. Mr. Slighcarp gave her a scowl and muttered something about putting her to mend sails or lipper the decks. Dido looked about for Mr. Pardon but saw that he was busy encouraging the men at the pumps while Nate, playing on a sort of zither made of whalebone, helped them keep time.

They were singing:

> "Strong to Pleasant, Wake to Guam,
>   Winds are favoring, seas are calm;
> Midway down to Pokaaku
>   Typhoon cuts our mainmast through.
>
> Easter, Disappointment, Nome,
>   Through the watery world we roam;
> Tristan, Fogo, Trinidad,
>   Winds contrary, weather bad;
> Christmas, Easter, Kwajalein—
>   When shall we see Brant Point again?"

The zither gave Dido an idea. There were bundles of whalebone pieces lying about the deck, of assorted sizes and shapes. "I reckon they can spare me a bit," she said to herself. "I won't bother to ask Cap'n Casket; he looks a mite cagged."

The captain was taking no part in the bustle; he

leaned against the mainmast with his eyes fixed on the far horizon.

Dido picked up a piece of bone about the size of a walking stick and quietly made off with it.

"Now all I want's a tool; land's sakes, they must have plenty on a ship this size—if I could find out where they keeps 'em."

There was a smith's forge by the foremast and a carpenter's bench aft of the tryworks, but both these were too much under observation at present; hoping to find other stores, Dido nipped down the forward hatchway into the blubber room. This was unoccupied now, and silent; a sort of tidemark on the wall showed where yesterday the blubber had been stacked knee-deep. At the moment, the room was being used for the temporary storage of things taken from the hold; a pile of oakum and sail canvas occupied most of the floor. Dido turned to leave, seeing nothing she could use, but then stopped, arrested by the unexpected sight of a boot protruding from under the canvas.

It was bottle green, elastic-sided, quite unlike the brogans worn by the sailors. It looked like an English lady's boot. Where could it have come from? Puzzled and inquisitive, Dido gave it a tug, and then jumped back with a yelp of alarm as the boot disappeared swiftly beneath the canvas. There was a foot inside it!

Curiosity overcoming her caution, Dido approached the heap once more and pulled aside some folds of canvas. A sort of writhing motion went on in the middle of the heap, the sailcloth was displaced, and suddenly, rather as a serpent darts out of its hole, the figure of a tall, veiled lady uncoiled and shot from under the pile of stuff. She towered over the quailing Dido, who would have run for it had she not been held fast by the ear.

"What are you doing here?" the lady said in a low, grating tone.

"P-p-please, ma'am, I d-didn't mean no harm!" gulped Dido. "I was only looking for a c-c-corkscrew!"

"A likely story! Prying and meddling where you'd no business to be! Repulsive child! You deserve to be severely punished. Now, listen here, miss!"

"Y-y-yes, ma'am?"

"If you so much as mention that you have seen me to anyone—anyone at all—I shall learn of it. And it will be the worse for you. You wish to return to England, do you not?"

"Yes, ma'am," Dido whispered, very much astonished.

"Then you had better keep a still tongue in your head! Otherwise, your chances of ever seeing London River again are very, very small. Do you understand? Now—go!"

Dido needed no encouragement—something in the veiled lady's aspect had struck her with mortal terror—but she received a final warning in the form of a box on the ear that shot her out of the doorway.

Numb and chattering with fright, she scurried up the companionway and back on deck. Luckily, nobody had noticed her come out. The whole crew were trying to manhandle a spare anchor out of its usual resting place so as to cram a few casks of oil underneath it. Frightened though she was, Dido kept her wits about her; she grabbed a handful of tools from the carpenter's bench and then, still gasping for breath, ran down to the captain's cabin.

She was too discomposed to notice that the closet door shut with a click as she entered the room, but she did observe, when a little more recovered, that the plum duff on the second plate had been eaten. She grinned to herself and, sitting up, inspected the tools she had taken. Choosing a drill, she set to work on her whalebone rod.

It proved a long, fiddling task, which occupied most of the day. Though aware that she was often watched, Dido pretended not to notice. Twice she broke off to make a tour of the room without touching the deck, each time attempting a new route. She also played several games of shuttlecock, and chalked herself out a hopscotch square on the chart table. Here she encountered a difficulty, however.

"I wisht as how I had a pebble," she remarked aloud. "Or a marble, or a penny, or even a button would do. Oh, well," she sighed, "I can't play hopscotch, that's all. Funny how I has a *fancy* to play hopscotch. Anyway, I reckon it's dinnertime; I'll nip up to the camboose and see what's cooking."

She took the empty plates and left the room.

All the time she had been working and playing, part of her mind was occupied with the puzzle of the mysterious veiled lady in the blubber room. Could she be a stowaway? She might have been hidden in the hold and obliged to take refuge elsewhere because of the general turnout. But where could she have come on board? What did she live on? Did none of the crew know about her presence?

"Somebody must know," Dido said to herself as she absently accepted two bowls of porpoise chowder from the cook. "*Somebody* must know, and musta told her about me. Else how did she twig I was English? I wonder who told her?"

She returned to the cabin, ate her meal, and flung herself on the bed for a nap, burying her face in the pillow and letting out snores. For a long time there was silence; then she heard a cautious clink. She redoubled her snores, shutting her eyes so tight that she saw red and green stars. At last, yawning loudly, she opened her eyes. The second chowder bowl was empty. Beside it lay a large leather button.

"Well, I never!" Dido exclaimed in astonishment. "Fancy my not noticing that there button afore! Jist what I needed for hopscotch! Now, can I remember the rules, I wonder?"

Having dumped the chowder bowls on the floor, she climbed onto the table. Addressing herself as if she were a slow-witted pupil, she proceeded to rehearse the rules of hopscotch, and then played it very enjoyably for an hour or so.

Tired of hopscotch, she set to work once more on the piece of whalebone. When this was hollowed into a tube, she made a series of holes along it and a mouthpiece. If blown on hard enough it produced a plaintive sound, like the call of a hungry bird. After much labor Dido had several notes adjusted to her satisfaction and was able to play "God Save King Jim" and "Who'll Buy My Sweet Lavender?" This was received with awe-struck and flattering silence from the watcher behind the panel.

"I wisht I knowed a few more tunes," Dido said at length. "Seems as how while I'd been asleep I forgot most o' the ones I used to know. Ah, well—maybe I'll remember some more tomorrow. I'll jist step out for a breath o' fresh air now, and then go to kip."

She went in search of Nate and found him sprawled on the main deck, weaving a rope mat in a rather inattentive and dreamy fashion while he hummed over the words of a chanty:

"Oh, it's gally and roll, me boys, ripple and run,
So hold to your hand lance, the chase has begun,
Tally-ho! till she breaches, come, join in the fun—
We're off on a Nantucket sleigh-ride.

It's flurry and scurry, she bolts and she sounds,
And something and something tum tiddle tum
grounds,
And something else ending in 'bounds' or in
'rounds'—
Hey ho! for a Nantucket sleigh-ride."

"Oh, hallo, chick," he broke off, on seeing Dido. "I've got summat for you. Finished it as soon as old man Slighcarp went below." And he brought out a beautiful little battledore, ingeniously made from woven strips of bone.

"Cool!" said Dido, "it's naffy! Ain't you clever? I'll lay Dutiful Pen won't be able to hold off when she sees this! Could you make another one, d'you reckon?"

"Guess so," Nate said agreeably. He started singing again:

"Tum tiddle tum tiddle tum tiddle tum grounds,
Pull on! head to head as his noddle he rounds..."

"Can you think of some rhymes for 'sounds,' chick?"

Dido could not. "Does you make 'em up, then?" she asked, much impressed.

"Sure. I allus used to make up verses at home, about sheep and funerals, you know, and pickled tamarinds and so forth, till my ma—she's a widder and so she gets fidgety—"

"Cagged, like?"

"I reckon so. She allowed as how I'd better go to sea before I drove her clean wild. So, as Uncle 'Lije was second mate with Cap'n Casket, he fixed it. They don't mind my verses on board ship; in fact, they come in quite handy."

Finding Nate such a kindred spirit, Dido showed him her whalebone pipe.

"That's cunning," he said, blowing on it. "Mighty smart work for a liddle 'un. Who learned you to do that?"

"My pa," Dido said proudly. "He plays on the hoboy, so he learned me how to make a tootlepipe."

"Say, we'll be able to have some fine concerts now when old Slighcarp's under hatches."

"It's time I was under hatches too," Dido remarked, looking up at the moon. And she added to herself, "I've a kind of a notion that Dutiful P. might surface tonight, so I'd best be there."

It had been an energetic day, with the hopscotch, the shuttlecock, the climbing, and hard work on the pipe; Dido turned out the lamp as soon as she reached the cabin, flung herself into the bed, and went straight to sleep.

About two hours later she found herself suddenly broad awake. The *Sarah Casket* was still speeding south before a following wind; Dido could feel the rush of the great seas as they lifted and drove past the ship's sides. Every timber creaked, and even down here the hum of wind in the rigging could be heard. Moonlight came through the ports; a patch of it on the floor hardly shifted, so steady was the ship on her course.

Dido wondered what had waked her.

Then she felt the clutch of little cold hands on her arm.

"Who is it?" she whispered.

"It's me. Dutiful Penitence."

"Ain't you cold, jist? Best come under the quilt, hadn't you?" Dido said matter-of-factly. She felt a small shape huddle up against her under the patchwork. Just at this moment the steersman evidently altered course a point or so, and the oblong of moonshine slid round, revealing the visitor.

She was a thin little creature, frail-looking as a cobweb (and no wonder, if she's been living on plum jelly ever since Santa Cruz, thought Dido), with long silvery hair, not very well brushed. She stared gravely at Dido.

"Are you really a girl?" she asked after a while.

"Yes, what d'you think? A mermaid?"

"But where did you come from?"

"Your pa picked me up, off the coast of England. I was in a ship what caught on fire and sank. And I've been asleep for ten months—so Nate says—all the time you was in storage."

"You were *in the sea?* Didn't you get scared?"

"It wasn't bad. I hung onto a mast."

"You must be brave! Are you English?"

"Yus. And don't I jist wish I was back in England,"

Dido remarked with feeling. "But your pa says he'll put me on a boat from New Bedford, wherever that is."

"Near Nantucket. We may unload there before going home. But I don't suppose I *shall* be going home now," Dutiful Penitence said drearily. "There'd be nobody to look after me except Aunt Tribulation, Papa says, and I won't stay with *her*. Dear Mamma would never have allowed it. Maybe Cousin Ann Allerton will have me in New Bedford."

"What's wrong with Aunt Tribulation?" Dido asked. She had heard the name before.

"She's Papa's sister. She's dreadfully sharp and unkind! She lives in Vine Rapids now, but she came to stay once and upset me and Mamma. Mamma would never let Papa invite her again; she said Aunt Tribulation was an *Amazon!* Oh, she did upset us! She said dear Mamma was a fool and was bringing me up to be a crybaby. And that my clothes were ridiculously fussy."

"What does she look like?"

"I can't remember—quite. It was a long time ago—when I was three. I remember she scolded me dreadfully because I was afraid of her dog. She said I was a little wet goose."

"What kind of dog was it?"

"A s-spaniel."

"Hum," said Dido. "For a sea captain's daughter you certainly are a rum 'un, Dutiful. Scared of a *spaniel?* And, look here, whoever tied that handle to you musta been dicked in the nob, and *I'm* not going to lay my tongue round it every time. I'll call you Pen. Agreeable?"

"Yes, thank you," Penitence said shyly. "No one

ever gave me a short name before. How old are you, Dido?"

"I've sorta lost count," Dido admitted. "With the long nap and all. Round about eleven, I reckon. What did you do all the time shut in that cupboard, Pen?"

"Oh, it wasn't bad. Come and see."

They lit the lamp, and Penitence showed Dido her little room. It was really a store cupboard with shelves all round, but one of them had been turned into a bunk. There were a few lesson books, writing materials, sewing things, and rows and rows of empty jelly bottles.

"I did lots of lessons," Penitence explained, "and I read the Bible and learned a hymn every day. Shall I say one?"

"Not jist now, thanks," Dido answered promptly. "Croopus, ain't you *good*, though? Didn't you never get fed up?"

"Oh, no. I kept a journal—but it wasn't very interesting," Penitence confessed. "And I worked on my sampler." She held up an extremely large square, embroidered in cross-stitch with a ship and whales and gulls and a long piece of poetry beginning, *"Myfterious Magnet! Ere thy ufe was known, Fear clad the Deep in horrors not itf own."* It was nearly finished.

"I'd sooner have done roses and doves," Penitence went on, "but dear M-Mamma thought it would please Papa if it had sea things. I began it when I was six."

"Well!" said Dido. "I'd ha' been blue-deviled in here. Specially when it's such prime fun on deck."

Penitence shivered. "I couldn't *bear* to go on deck. That dreadful sea! I know I'd fall in! And all the

cross, rough men, and the horrid smells and dirt.
Mamma always said it was dangerous up there. You
won't try to make me go, will you?"

"Bless you, no. It ain't my affair. Anyhows, we can
have a bang-up time in the cabin now you've decided
to come out and be civil."

"Will you teach me that game with the feathered
thing? And play tunes on your pipe?"

"Course I will. Us'll have rare fun."

"You don't think Mamma would mind?" Penitence
said hesitantly. "She said playing games was a sin."

"Croo—" Dido began, but bit the words back.

Her own parents, as she recalled, had never seemed
particularly kind or fond of her, but at least they
were quite *sensible;* all that was said of Mrs. Casket,
however, seemed to suggest that the woman had been
an utter fool. Musta been queer in her attic, Dido
thought. "Reckon she knows better now?" she suggested gruffly. "Lawks, if you never played, what *did* you
do at home?"

"Helped with the housework."

"Well, I done that too. But I played arterward."

"After I'd done my tasks, Mamma used to let me sit
on her lap while she read the Bible," said Penitence.
Her composure faltered. "If—if I'd been extra good
she used—she used to sing a h-hymn—"

Here, breaking down altogether, Penitence threw
herself on the bed, buried her head in the quilt, and
cried. She cried very much indeed.

Dido looked at her worriedly. There was little con-
solation to offer. Foolish, Mrs. Casket may have been,
but her daughter had plainly thought the world of
her.

"Don't take on so," Dido said after a while, with

awkward sympathy. "Want a hankersniff? I've got one."

But as Penitence made no reply, just went on crying and shivering and choking, Dido knelt down on the floor by her, feeling oddly grown-up and capable and protective, and put an arm round her.

"Cheer up," she muttered. "I'll keep an eye on you. It won't work out so bad. You'll see."

The small, silvery head rubbed against her.

"Will you? Will you really?"

"That I will."

"And when we get home to Nantucket? Will you stay with me then? So's Papa don't leave me all alone with Aunt Tribulation? Please? *Please!* Mamma once said she couldn't bear for me to be brought up by Aunt Tribulation. She said Aunt Tribulation was a T-T-Tartar!"

The thin arms came round Dido's neck in a tight hug, so that she could hardly breathe.

"Well—maybe," Dido said reluctantly. "Just for a little while. Till your pa gets you fixed up with somebody else—"

"Oh, you are kind! You're so much braver than I am. I'm scared of *everything*. But you've even been in the *sea!* If you'll—if you'll stay with me it will be much better. Will you promise?"

"All right," Dido said, sighing.

"Would you—would you sing something now? That song you were singing before?"

"All right," said Dido again. She began to sing in a small gruff voice:

"Who'll buy my sweet lavender?
Three bunches a penny!

*Fresh picked in Sevenoaks this morning,
Three bunches a penny!"*

She stroked the tousled head. It lay heavily on her shoulder, and before long drooped in sleep.

Dido sat and stared at the lamp, which they had forgotten to turn out. Presently its yellow flame swelled and wavered in a blur of tears. Resolutely she blinked them away. It was stupid to be homesick. But she longed for the familiar London streets where she had played. With a heavy heart she wondered how long it would be before she saw them again.

"I'll tell you one thing, Pen, my girl," she muttered as the sleeping Penitence shifted against her. "If I'm to look arter you, I'm somehow going to get you out o' this way o' being scairt o' the whole blame world!"

CHAPTER FOUR

Encouraging Pen. The Galapagos. Gamming with the
Martha. Mr. Slighcarp's strange behavior. Round the
Horn and back to New Bedford.

"Psst! Hey! Cap'n—Cap'n Casket! Will you step
thisaway?"

Captain Casket started, as Dido's voice roused him
from his usual sad reverie; he turned and saw her
standing behind him.

Making sure that no one could overhear, she came
close to him and hissed conspiratorially, "I've done it!
She's out!"

Captain Casket appeared thunderstruck.

"On deck?"

"No, no, no, gaffer. Not yet. Give us time. But she's
out in the cabin eatin' of plum duff and a-playin'
hopscotch. I'll have her on deck one o' these days,
though, s'long as you don't come creating and badger-
ing."

"Thee is a remarkable child," Captain Casket said
solemnly.

"I say, though," Dido went on, "what 'bout this
Auntie Trib, then? She fair gives young Pen the hor-

rors. It'll be all my work for Habakkuk if Pen finds
Auntie Trib's going to have charge of her in Nantucket; she'll snib herself up in the pantry again before you can say whale-o!"

Captain Casket looked harassed. "Sister Tribulation
is really a most estimable character," he murmured.
"She is endowed with every Christian virtue."

"You allus says that," Dido objected.

"My poor Sarah—my poor wife never understood
her. But I am sure that *thee* could persuade Dutiful
Penitence to like her aunt, my child."

"That's as may be," Dido said doubtfully. "Anyhows, you better consider if there ain't somebody else
as could do the job. I'm a-warning you, see. Goodness
sakes, on an island the size of Nantucket" (Dido had
found it on the map by now) "there must be somebody else as could have charge of her. Between what
Pen thinks she remembers and what her ma said
about Auntie Trib, she's fair frit o' the name 'Tribulation.' Now I'm a-going to teach Dutiful P. to play
shuttlecock; lor, I don't wonder the poor little thing's
so mopish. She ain't had no upbringing at all!"

It took several weeks of Dido's company and encouragement before Penitence could be persuaded on
deck. Dido was too shrewd to hurry her. They played
endless games in the cabin, sang songs, asked riddles,
and talked, each telling the other the whole story of
her life. Penitence was quite amazed by Dido's
homesick tales of the London streets and could never
hear enough about the fairs and the fights, the street
markets, Punch and Judy shows, glimpses of grand
people in their carriages, and the little Scottish King
James III, against whom the Hanoverians were always plotting.

"Fancy living in such a great city!" Penitence said dreamily. "Why, where we lived in Nantucket it's almost three miles to the next *house*."

"Wouldn't suit me," Dido said. "I likes a bit o' life and company. There was allus summat doing in Rose Alley, London, where I come from." She sighed, thinking of it.

"My mamma didn't like the loneliness either. She came from Boston. When Papa went to sea," Pen confessed, "she used to take me for long visits to Cousin Ann in New Bedford and Aunt Edith in Boston. We never stayed in Nantucket very long, and I haven't been there for years. Mamma was scared of being on her own."

"I wouldn't be *scared;* not such a clodpole as that," Dido said. "Just prefer more people about. Don't you want to write your journal now, Pen? And learn a hymn or two? Tol-lol. I'll go up on deck for a breath of air."

Dido had become quite fond of Pen by now—there was more in the funny little thing than met the eye—but, nonetheless, it was a relief to run up on deck now and then, to talk to Nate and joke with the sailors; after a few hours of Pen's company she felt she wanted to shout and jump and climb into the rigging. Pen had grown absolutely devoted to her and, Dido considered, was coming out of her mopey ways very well. By innumerable tales about her own life Dido was managing to suggest that *all* dogs do not bite, that occupations such as skating and swimming can be enjoyable, that people tend to be friendlier when you talk to them boldly and cheerfully than when you cower away as if you expect them to murder you. Progress was being made.

Pen still kept her quiet tastes, though; she liked to spend several hours a day doing lessons and sewing; she offered to read the Bible or hymns to Dido, but this, for the most part, Dido politely refused.

"Tell you what, though," she suggested. "How 'bout asking your pa if we can invite Nate to come down and sing you some o' his songs? He knows a rare lot, and on top o' that he's allus rattling off new ones. Wouldn't you like it, eh?"

Penitence looked doubtful. "I haven't seen Nate since he was twelve. Is he very big now? He isn't rough? He wouldn't tease me or hurt me?"

"Now, *Pen!* Don't you know me better'n that by now? Would I ask him if he was liable to do such blame-fool things? I'm *surprised* at you!"

Pen apologized and recalled that Nate's mother had been very kind and used to bring her presents of bantam eggs when she was little. Captain Casket's permission was obtained, and Nate, rather bashfully, came down to the stateroom with his zither. At first Penitence trembled a good deal at the close presence of such a tall, lanky, red-headed creature, and was quite speechless with shyness. But when Nate sang:

> *"Oh, fierce is the Ocean and wild is the Sound,*
> *But the isle of Nantucket is where I am bound—*
> *Sweet isle of Nantucket! where the grapes are so*
>   *red,*
> *And the light flashes nightly on Sankaty Head!"*

she was quite delighted, clapped her hands, and exclaimed, "Oh that *is* pretty! Sing it again!"

Nate sang it again, and many others. Dido, curled up under the chart table, hugged her knees and congratulated herself. From that day, Nate was a welcome visitor in the cabin; in fact, he was with them, singing a song about the high-rolling breakers on the south shore of Nantucket, and the brave fishermen who launched their dories through the foam, when a sudden shout from the deck startled them.

"Land! Land-ho!"

"Must have sighted the Galapagos!" said Nate, scrambling to his feet. "Blame it, why wasn't I up aloft? Cap'n Casket allus gives half a dollar to the first one that sights land. See you later, gals!" And he bolted out.

"How about it, Pen," Dido said carelessly. "Coming ashore for a look-see? Nate says there are giant tortoises on the Galapagos, as big as tea tables."

Penitence quailed. "Do they bite?"

"Pen, you really are a jobberknoll! How could a poor old tortoise bite you? He can't go much faster than a snail."

Pen hesitated in an agony of indecision. She longed to set foot on firm ground, but she was terrified of the frail, tippy boat in which they would have to be rowed to shore.

"I'd better change into my deck dress, hadn't I?" she said doubtfully.

"Deck dress? What in thunder's that?"

"Mamma always made me do so." Pen fetched it from a drawer. It was made of black taffeta, with many frills.

"Dear knows how you'd climb the rigging in *that*," Dido said with disfavor.

"Climb the *rigging*?" Pen turned pale at the very thought. "I'm not going to climb the rigging!"

"Oh, poison!" exclaimed Dido. "Change, then, if

you want to. Only be quick about it. I must say, those togs you're wearing is a bit on the jammy side, now I comes to look at 'em. Maybe it *is* time you changed. Come on, I'll do you up the back."

There were about thirty tiny buttons on each of Pen's dresses; by the time Dido had undone one lot and done up the others, fiddling with the exquisitely stitched little satin loops, more than half an hour had gone by. The chance was lost: the boat had already set off for shore, under the command of Mr. Slighcarp, to secure fresh stocks of water and vegetables. Dido was bitterly disappointed but tried to conceal it because she had soon discovered that if she seemed put out, Pen flinched and showed a tendency to retreat into the cupboard again. So she swallowed her regret and said, "Never mind. Let's go up and see what we can see."

In fact, Dido was quite glad of the chance to bring Pen on deck while Mr. Slighcarp was out of the way; the rest of the men were kind and friendly to her, but the first mate always greeted her with a scowl and a harsh word; she had been rather anxious about the effect of this on Penitence. Luckily, the deck was quite empty when, clutching Dido's hand in a tight grip, Penitence timidly followed her up the companionway and came blinking into the sunshine.

"Oh," she breathed in astonishment. "Isn't it *bright!* And warm! I thought we were in the Arctic."

"We left that behind weeks ago," Dido said kindly. "Sit down on a coil o' rope; you're all of a tremble."

Penitence sank down obediently. In the bright sunshine her face seemed as pale as a primrose, and contrasted strangely with Dido's healthy tan. At first she was pitiably nervous; her great blue eyes widened and she clasped Dido's hand violently whenever a wave crest broke near the ship. The land was too far away for much to be visible except a low-lying mass with some scrubby trees on it. But they were excited to see another ship, the *Martha*, anchored not far away.

Presently Captain Casket wandered along the deck towards them. He started uncontrollably when he saw Penitence, but Dido gave him such a fierce scowl of warning that he tried to conceal his astonishment and only said, "I am glad to see thee out in the fresh air at last, Daughter. Thee must get some roses into thy cheeks like those of thy little friend."

Penitence made an awkward bob and answered, "Yes, Papa," in such a subdued tone that it was hardly audible; she seemed greatly relieved when he walked away along the deck.

"You don't seem very pleased to see your pa, Pen," Dido remarked. "What's wrong? Ain't you fond of him? He's not a bad old codger. I wish *my* pa had ever said he was glad to see me!"

"Oh, yes—I am f-fond of Papa," Penitence faltered. "Only—only he always looks so gloomy and s-stern that he s-scares me dreadfully!"

Dido heaved a great sigh. "Dutiful Penitence Casket! Is there a single solitary thing that you *ain't* scared of?"

Soon there came a hail from the *Martha*, and a boat was lowered and rowed towards them; a cheerful, red-faced man called, "Jabez! Cap'n Jabez Casket! Are you there? Can I come aboard for a gam? I've some mail for you, only eight months out o' New Bedford."

"Come aboard and welcome, Cap'n Bilger," Captain Casket called, and the skipper of the *Martha* was

swung aboard in the captain's chair. He handed over
a batch of letters for the *Sarah Casket's* captain and
crew, and asked if they could spare any ship's biscuit,
as most of his had been spoiled by a leak; he offered
coffee and lemon syrup in exchange (which the cook
was glad to accept, since Pen had eaten all the jelly).

"Consarn it!" exclaimed Captain Bilger, slapping
his leg suddenly in annoyance. "If I haven't forgotten
to bring over that blame bird!"

"Bird? What bird?" Captain Casket inquired.

"Why, a bird belonging to that boy of yours, Nate
Pardon. One of my men caught it flapping about the
streets of New Bedford before we sailed, and recognized it as his; we've had it aboard ever since. I'll be
thankful to see the last of it, I can tell you. That bird
would talk the ears off a brass monkey. Now I come
to think, I've another letter for you, as well. It got a
mite damp, came unstuck, and I put it aside from the
others. My memory's fuller of holes'n a dip net."

"No matter," said Captain Casket. "My men can
call round by the *Martha* when they come back from
provisioning and pick up the bird and the letter.
Young Nate will be glad to see his pet."

The two captains went below to gossip and, an
early tropical dusk falling soon after, Dido and Penitence also retired to their cabin to play Hunt the
Thimble and speculate as to what sort of things
Nate's bird would be able to say.

Pen was quite tired out by the fresh air and the excitement of being on deck; she soon went to bed and
to sleep. Dido, however, was not sleepy; she returned
to lean on the rail and gaze wistfully at the lights on
shore. Presently she heard Captain Bilger taking his
leave.

"By the way, has thee heard anything of the pink whale?" Captain Casket inquired. "I was on her track at the beginning of this voyage, but we lost her while rounding the Horn."

"Pink whale? Old Rosie Lee? I should just about think we have," Captain Bilger said laughing. Evidently, all his friends knew of Captain Casket's fancy. "A batch of Indios told my first mate she'd been sighted off the coast of Peru—only *they* called her the Greak Pink Sea Serpent. Maybe she's on the watch for your ship, old friend—heard that you were looking for her. But it's *my* belief those Indios had taken a drop too much prickly-pear juice."

"Thee did not go after her?" Captain Casket's tone betrayed anxiety.

"No, no," Captain Bilger said. "Not I. To tell truth, I reckon your pink whale is more of a wild goose. I don't believe in her above half."

"But I myself am nearly certain that I saw her—off Madeira. Only I never drew close enough to be sure—"

"Indigestion," Captain Bilger said. "Too much pepper in the lobscouse!"

He waved cheerfully and went over the side in the captain's chair, still laughing.

Later on, the men returned. Having been instructed by lantern signals, they rowed round by the *Martha* and picked up Nate's bird, but no extra letter. Dido heard Mr. Slighcarp reporting that there had been a mistake over this: Captain Bilger had found that the letter was addressed to the captain of some other ship.

Captain Casket nodded vaguely, hardly troubling to listen to this explanation; he seemed excited and preoccupied. But Dido, squatting on the quarterdeck,

thought Mr. Slighcarp's manner very odd: he had a
sly, pleased look, as if something had turned out very
much to his advantage. And just before reporting to
Captain Casket he had thrust some white object under his jacket. What could it be? What was he up to?

Nate was overjoyed to recover his bird, which he
had never expected to see again, and showed it off
proudly to Dido.

"His name's 'Mr. Jenkins.' Ain't he beautiful?"

Dido admired the bird's glossy black plumage and
brilliant yellow bill. "He's naffy! Where'd you get
him, Nate?"

"Bought him off'n a British sailor in Fayal. I've
had him three years."

"What does he say?"

The bird gave her a haughty glance and remarked,
"Dinner is served in the small ballroom, Your Grace."

"Ain't he a stunner?" Nate said. "He goes on like
that all the time. I reckon as how he musta belonged
to some lord or duke once in England, and someone
maybe stole him. I'm right pleased to get him back. A
cat scared him when I was carrying him in New Bedford and he flew off my shoulder; I couldn't find him
before we sailed."

"Order the perch phaeton," croaked Mr. Jenkins.
"A young person has called, Your Lordship. Tea is
served in Her Grace's boudoir. Ho, there, a chair for
Lady Fothergill!"

"You silly old sausage," said Nate, giving his pet a
loving hug. "There aren't any lords or dukes here."

Affronted and on his dignity, Mr. Jenkins clambered out of Nate's arms and ascended to the top of
his head, where he suddenly shouted in a stentorian
voice: "God save the King! Horray for Jamie Three!

God save our sovereign lord King James and DOWN WITH THE GEORGIANS!"

Mr. Slighcarp happened to be passing at that moment. He gave a violent start and dropped the telescope he was carrying. It fell with a crash.

"Who was that?" he cried.

"It was the bird, Mr. Slighcarp, old Jenkins."

"Well, don't let him do it again, or I'll wring his neck!" the mate said with an oath. "Plague take the creature. You'd best keep him under hatches if he's liable to go on like that. I won't have it, see!"

Much abashed, Nate hurried his pet below. Dido, who was still feeling wakeful, retreated to a patch of shadow against the bulwards and curled up there, listening longingly to cheerful sounds of music and singing from the *Martha*.

Presently Captain Casket approached her. He was a changed man since hearing tidings of the pink whale; his eyes glittered feverishly and he walked with a rapid, excited step.

"Ah, my child," he said cordially, "is not this stirring news?"

Dido thought he was referring to the mail he had received.

"You fixed up what you're going to about young Pen, then, when you gets back to Nantucket?" she said hopefully. "Someone offered to look arter her?"

"Oh, that. No, no I was referring to the news that the pink whale has been sighted off the Peruvian coast. We shall see her! I feel certain that we shall see her soon!"

"Oh, bother the pink whale," Dido said testily. "What about Pen?"

"Ah yes. I had a letter from dear Tribulation. She

writes with true sisterly feeling, having just heard of my poor wife's death. She will move to Nantucket and look after Dutiful Penitence and the house for me."

"But, blame it!" Dido said in exasperation. "Pen don't *want* to live with her Auntie Tribulation! That won't answer at *all!* Pen's ma said Aunt Trib was a Tartar, and it's my belief Pen thinks that's summat that eats children for breakfast."

"Tribulation suggests further," Captain Casket went on, dreamily looking out over the water and ignoring Dido, "that a companion, some other girl of her age, would be an advantage for Penitence, since my farm, Soul's Hill, is situated in a somewhat lonely location. So if thee will accept the charge, my child— not for very long, of course—that will solve all our problems, will it not? Thy quick wit will soon smooth over any little difficulties between my daughter and her good aunt. And when Penitence is settled and happy, my sister Tribulation will no doubt see that thee is found a passage to England."

"Oh, for the love of fish!" Dido exclaimed. "Don't you know young Pen's scared to *death* of her aunt? Settled and happy? That wouldn't be till pigs went on roller skates. I'll never get home at that rate. There must be *someone* else in Nantucket as'd take her. Don't you know of *nobody?*"

Captain Casket fixed his large eyes on her and said, mildly but with dignity, "I know that my sister Tribulation is a good, devout woman."

"Endowed with every Christian virtue," muttered Dido.

"And I know, also, that we rescued thee from the

sea, my child, and that thee owes us a debt of gratitude."

Bottled and silenced, Dido knit her brow as he walked away. "Never mind how devout Auntie Trib may be," she said to herself. "*That* won't cut much ice if she frightens the poor little brat. Still, it's true Pen's got some rare, rummy notions and hasn't seen the old girl since she was three. Maybe Aunt Trib's not so bad as she's painted. We'll have to see, I reckon." She sighed rather despondently.

An hour or so went by and Dido was about to retire, when she noticed the figure of Mr. Slighcarp standing not far away. Something furtive and cautious about his manner attracted her interest, and she watched him sharply as he made his way to the rail. Unaware of Dido, squatting motionless in the shadows, Mr. Slighcarp looked quickly all round him and then proceeded to tear in tiny pieces some sheets of paper which he had carried hidden in the breast of his jacket, and drop them over the side.

"What's he doing that for?" wondered Dido. "What's so tarnation private that he don't want no one to see it?"

Then she recalled that Mr. Slighcarp had been asked to collect a letter for the captain, and that he had not done so. He had said Captain Bilger had made a mistake, the letter was for somebody else. But he had stuffed something white under his jacket in a stealthy, suspicious way. Could it have been the letter? Had he lied about it and kept it, instead of giving it to Captain Casket? Suppose this was it? But why do such a thing? And why should he be destroying it now?

There seemed no answer to this puzzle, or none

that Dido could supply. She continued to watch Mr.
Slighcarp attentively, however, and was somewhat astonished by what he did next. Making sure, as he
thought, that he was unobserved, he produced a pair
of boots from under his jacket, and brushed them
long and carefully.

Dido's heart beat fast and she nodded to herself
grimly.

A brilliant tropical moon swam overhead, and by
its light every detail of the scene was clearly visible.
The boots that Mr. Slighcarp brushed were no sailors'
brogans but a pair of English ladies' buttoned trav-
eling boots in dull bottle green.

At last, satisfied, apparently, with the appearance
of the boots, Mr. Slighcarp retired once more, in the
same prudent and furtive manner.

Dido remained on deck for a considerable time
longer. At first she had half a mind to tell Captain
Casket about the incident. But then she decided not
to. After all, what had she to go on but suspicion?
Who could say that the letter was not Mr. Slighcarp's
own? He had every right to tear up his own letter.
Furthermore, if Mr. Slighcarp realized that Dido had
seen him tear it up, he would know that she had also
seen him brushing the boots. He would be revealed as
the accomplice of the stowaway lady in the blubber
room. Dido had not forgotten this lady's fiercely whispered threat: "Keep a still tongue in your head, or
your chances of ever seeing London River again are
very, very small!"

"I'll keep mum," she finally decided. "After all, if I
did tell Captain Casket, like as not he'd only gaze at
me in that moon-faced way o' his and start to talk
about his everlasting pink whale. I daresay it wasn't

his letter. And I don't want an up-and-a-downer with old man Slighcarp. I'll keep a still tongue. But I'll watch."

Nate, whose turn it was on the middle watch, came on deck at this moment and passed the time of night with Dido. Mr. Jenkins, sitting on his shoulder, gave a polite croak and remarked, "Your Lordship's bath is ready in the tapestry room. I have warmed the morning paper, Sir Henry. Pray bring His Grace's bath chair this way. Down with the scurvy Hanoverians!"

"Best watch out for Mr. Slighcarp," Dido said, grinning.

"No danger; it's his watch below," Nate said. "That's why I brought old Jenkins up for a breath of air."

"I wonder why he riles Mr. Slighcarp so," Dido said yawning.

"Don't you know? It's because Mr. Slighcarp's an English Hanoverian himself. D'you know about them?"

"Oh, yes," Dido said. "My uncle's a Hanoverian, I know all about 'em. They don't like the king we got on the throne, Jamie Three. They want to push him off and have a prince that lives over in Hanover, the one they call 'Bonnie Prince Georgie,' instead. There's a song about it: *My bonnie lives over in Hanover. Oh, why won't they bring that young man over?* Some calls 'em Hanoverians, some calls 'em Georgians. They keeps plotting away, but they're allus caught afore the plan comes to anything. Then they're sent to jail unless they can get away overseas."

"Yes, that's it," Nate said. "Mr. Slighcarp wanted to blow up your King James III, Uncle 'Lije told me, and he was nearly caught and had to run abroad in a hurry or he'd a'been clapped in prison. The militia was after him. So that's why he don't like it when the old bird says 'Down with the Hanoverians!' "

"Fancy Mr. Slighcarp being a Hanoverian," Dido said. "Has he shipped with you long?"

"Only this trip. But he stayed in Nantucket a piece before that. You'd think he'd taken more of a shine to you," Nate remarked. "Seeing you both come from the same part."

But Dido was hardly attending. She said goodnight and went below, plunged in thought. What was the connection between Mr. Slighcarp and the stowaway lady, who had spoken with an English accent too? Was she another Hanoverian, escaping overseas?

It was a long time, almost dawn, before Dido fell asleep, and when she did so her slumbers were soon broken short by a sudden and violent disturbance.

The whole ship seemed to give a tremendous bound, like a startled horse; there were loud and prolonged cries overhead; feet thudded on the deck, and Dido heard the crash and rattle as sails were shaken out and the anchor was dragged bodily from the bottom.

"What's the matter? What's happened?" Pen cried fearfully—she had been jerked out of bed by the ship's unexpected movement and was whimpering on the floor. "Is it a hurricane?"

Dido held up a hand for silence. She was listening attentively to the tumult.

"No," she said dryly after a minute, "it ain't a hurricane; a little thing like that wouldn't get your pa so stirred up."

"Oh! We're sailing!" Pen said in dismay as an unexpected pitch sent her sliding across the floor. "I hoped we were going to stay here at anchor for several days."

"So did I. We was wrong, warn't we?" Dido agreed, picking Pen up and shaking her to rights before putting her back on the bed. "Steady there, Dutiful! I guess you'd better stop where you are till things ease off, while I go and rustle up a bit o' prog. Shan't be long."

When she came back, with some slices of breadfruit, and a bowl of lemon syrup, she nodded grimly to Pen's inquiring look.

"Jist what I thought," she remarked. "Oh, well, one thing—it'll help us on our way home at a rattling good pace. That is, allus supposing the old gal plays her part and don't go skedaddling off to Timbuctoo or Tobaygo."

"How do you mean? What old gal?"

"Why," Dido said, "the pink 'un. Rosie Lee. Your pa's fancy. We're a-chasin' after that there sweet-pea-colored whale of hisn."

The days and weeks that followed were fierce and rugged. Careering after her quarry through the South Pacific trades, the *Sarah Casket* flew along under every sail that she would take. Maintops, top-gallants, and stunsails were set; the rigging thrummed like a banjo; and often, as they drove through the southern seas, their mainmast was bent over so far that Nate declared they might as well use it for a bow, if they ever got close enough to the pink whale, and fire off a harpoon from the mainstay.

Nothing would persuade Penitence to come on deck now, and even Dido, when they reached the wild easterlies and heavy squalls in the Straits of Magellan, was glad enough to stay in the cabin playing parcheesi.

At first Dido was inclined, like the others, to believe that Captain Casket had merely imagined his glimpse of the pink whale at Galapagos, until one evening, south of Cape Horn, she saw something between two wildly blowing williwaws that she at first took to be a momentary view of the setting sun—except that it lay to the east. It was like a rosy, iridescent bubble balanced amid the black, leaping seas. Then the storm came down again, and they saw it no more. But Captain Casket, with a frantic, exultant light in his eye, kept the ship under full press of canvas, heedless of danger, clapping on new sails as the old ones ripped away. Without regard to tempest, tidal wave, or terremote, he fought his way round the Horn, making a record passage of it, while his men served four hours on and four off, becoming haggard and thin from wear and tear and lack of sleep. The captain himself never seemed to sleep at all, and his eyes were red from scanning the horizon.

There were few chances for Nate to come down to the cabin now; he was kept busy all the time as a lookout, or taking soundings, or mending the tattered sails. Sometimes he could be heard singing as he sewed, with Mr. Jenkins (who had acquired a wholesome respect for Mr. Slighcarp) supplying the chorus in a subdued croak:

"Stow your line tubs, belay tail feathers,
It's rough, it's rugged, it's blowy weather.
Make your passage and follow the moon—
Dinner is served in the blue saloon.

Slush the spars and splice the rigging,
Leave your scrimshaw and grab your piggin.
Bail, boys, bail! for your wage and lay—
Her Ladyship's carriage blocks the way."

Mr. Jenkins spent a good deal of this time in the cabin. The girls were glad of his company, as he made an extremely civil guest. He would play tiddly-winks (if ever they struck a long enough patch of calm weather), flipping scrimshaw counters into a cup with great dexterity and enjoyment, while his grave observations about life in high society kept Pen and Dido amused for hours.

Past the Falklands they chased, past the Brazilian coast, through the Sargasso Sea (which slowed down the pink whale a little, for she got weeds caught in her flukes), past Bermuda, past Cape Hatteras, and so home. But the pink whale, unfortunately, seemed dis-inclined to stop, and mutterings were to be heard among the men that at this rate they'd likely be skat-ing past Newfoundland before they discharged cargo and had their pay.

A deputation waited on Captain Casket and pointed out to him that they were low on stores and water, that there wasn't a single unmended sail on board, and that what hardtack was left would walk away from you along the deck if you let go of your ra-tion for a moment. With great difficulty, he was per-suaded to put in to New Bedford.

And so it was that, almost seven months to the day after she had first opened her eyes on board the *Sarah Casket*, Dido had a chance to set foot on solid ground.

"New Bedford!" she said ungratefully. "Where's

that, I ask you? Land sakes, Cap'n Casket mighta just as well nipped across to London. It wouldn't 'a taken him but a few more weeks."

She glared with disfavor at the trim roofs of the town climbing the hill above the harbor. "Still," she admitted in acknowledgment of the forest of masts, "I *will* say there's plenty of shipping here; maybe I'll find me some bark as'll take me on to England."

"You promised you'd come home with me first, you *promised*," Pen reminded her anxiously.

"All right, all right, I ain't forgotten," Dido growled. "I've said I'll see you right, and I will—if we can only get your pa to tend to your affairs for two minutes together. You know you had a notion your cousin, Ann Allerton, might put you up."

Captain Casket hardly even attended to the business of getting his ship safely docked. His eyes were constantly turned back towards the open sea, and his thoughts were all with the pink whale, who had unfairly taken the chance to nip off round Cape Cod and into the Gulf of Maine. Would he ever catch up with her again?

It was dark before the *Sarah Casket* was alongside the wharf and made fast. Penitence begged to go ashore then and there, but Captain Casket wouldn't hear of disturbing Cousin Ann Allerton so late in the evening, and left them to spend one more night on board. Dido stayed awake for hours, sniffing the land smells, listening to the shouts and the splash of oars in the harbor and the cry of gulls, and the music coming from the sailors' taverns. She dragged a chair to the port and squatted there looking out at the lights as they gradually dimmed and died along the wharfside and in the streets above the warehouses.

Strangely enough, although she was now nearer home than she had been for the last year, she felt more lonely and homesick than ever before. The sight of roofs and lights, the noise of wheels on cobbles reminded her almost unbearably of Rose Alley in London town.

"Pen!" she whispered after a while. "Hey, Dutiful! Are you awake?"

The only answer was soft, even breathing. Dido sighed and was about to climb down from her perch and go to bed, when she heard a faint splash, close to, and the creak of oars. Turning back, she was just in time to see Mr. Slighcarp, his foxy features visible in the light of a lantern, help a tall, veiled woman over the *Sarah Casket's* side into a dory, and row quietly away across the harbor.

CHAPTER FIVE

Trouble with Cousin Ann. Captain Casket slips his
cable. Arrival in Nantucket. The Casket farm.

"WE CAN'T stay with your cousin Allerton," Dido said
glumly. "And *that's* for sure."

It had taken her less than ten minutes to reach this
conclusion.

Cousin Ann Allerton was a frail, erect old lady
dressed in black silk with a white bib and cap. She almost fainted when her snapping black eyes first took
in the untidy appearance of the two girls—even Pen's
deck dress was fairly bedraggled by this time with oil
and tar on its frills. And as for Dido—!

"Don't stand on the clean doormat!" Cousin Ann
said frantically. "Keziah! Keziah! fetch an old sheet
directly and put on a pail of water to heat. Mercy!
just look at that child's feet! And her *hair!* Bring
some towels—every stitch they have on will have to be
burned. Get out the tallow and kerosene—gracious
knows how we are going to get that grease off. Fetch
the sulphur and calomel—I don't doubt they need a
good dose after eating dear knows what foreign truck

on board ship. And when you've done that, run down the road and ask Miss Alsop to step up, they'll have to have everything new, I can see that—furs, flannels, merinos, poplins, and tarlatans. Bonnets, of course, and boots; mercy on us, what a pair of little savages!"

"I'd druther keep my britches," Dido said, scowling.

"Quiet, child! The *idea!* Pass me the bath brick, Keziah, so I can give them a good scrubbing."

Dido had never been treated so in her life before and was almost too thunderstruck to protest; in no time they were put to bed in a spotlessly neat bedroom with white chintz curtains and fringed white dimity bedcovers, a braided rug exactly in the middle of the floor, and a square of oilcloth in front of the washstand.

"Why've we got to go to bed in daytime?" grumbled Dido. "We ain't done nothing wrong!"

"Oh, for the land's sake, will you hold your hush. You must stay out of sight of the neighbors till you've something fit to wear."

Miss Alsop, the dressmaker, soon arrived, and with Cousin Ann's help, two brown calico dresses trimmed with white tape were hastily run up so that the children might put them on, get out of bed, and help to hem some more garments.

"I won't stand for it," Dido muttered again and again, wriggling her neck furiously in her starched collar as she sewed under Cousin Ann's gimlet-eyed supervision. The only respite they had from sewing was when the gaunt and gloomy maid, Keziah, compelled them to swallow another dose of rhubarb or senna or sassafras tea; Cousin Ann seemed quite certain that they had brought the plague with them from abroad and must be physicked at frequent intervals to prevent it from spreading through the town.

There seemed no escape from the torment. They were never allowed out by themselves, and so could not visit the ship and complain to Captain Casket; nor, for ten days, did they see anything of him. He was so absorbed in refitting the *Sarah Casket* with all possible speed that he had entirely forgotten their existence. When he did finally remember them, he reluctantly tore himself away from the wharf to call at the Allerton house for half an hour. He was mildly surprised at the transformation which had been wrought in the two children, when he caught a glimpse of them through Cousin Ann's parlor window. They were sitting on the back porch, enduring as well as they could a lesson in drawn-thread work from sharp Miss Alsop.

"Penitence looks almost as she did when her dear mother was alive," Captain Casket remarked, sighing. "Thee has done wonders, Cousin Ann."

"I hope you're not expecting me to keep 'em for good, Jabez?" Cousin Ann returned sharply. "It was one thing for the child to visit here when she was a little thing and that poor Sarah of yours was alive to look after her. It would be quite another to have her now. And as for that other heathen girl I declare they make me quite nervous, the pair of them; I should always be expecting to find the house burnt over my head."

She glanced grimly at the two children sitting on their upright chairs.

"No, no, I thank thee, Cousin Ann," Captain Casket said mildly. "My sister Tribulation said she would be in Nantucket by now. She will look after them."

"Hmm—well, that *may* answer," sniffed Cousin Ann. "Tribulation should be able to keep them in order. Why didn't she call on me if she's in Nantucket? She must have passed through New Bedford on her way. Downright uncivil, I call it."

Captain Casket took his leave as soon as possible; he was on tenterhooks to get back to the ship. The children did not even see him until he was at the end of the road.

"Quick!" Dido said then—Miss Alsop had gone indoors for more thread—"Let's go arter him and tell him we can't stick it here."

"But Cousin Ann says we must not go farther than the end of the road!"

"Well, nuts to Cousin Ann. What does she think we'll do, get lost in this one-horse town?"

It was fine summer weather, with a fresh smell of lilac and honeysuckle. Cousin Ann lived in a big yellow-and-white house, set well back from the sidewalk in a quiet street, with a thick privet hedge on either side.

"Ain't it slow here," Dido said, looking about the peaceful, sunny neighborhood with disapproval. "Dull, I calls it. Not a patch on dear old London. Don't I just wish I was there! Come on, I dessay your pa's gone back to the harbor. Let's run!"

She dashed down the hill, impatiently hitching up her brown calico skirts, with Penitence in anxious pursuit. But they had only just come in sight of the *Sarah Casket*, where refitting was already well under way, when they were overtaken by the dour Keziah, who boxed their ears and marched them back to Cousin Ann's house. There they received another scolding and an extra large dose, a fearsome one, of

salts, pennyroyal, and ginger balsam, all mixed together, "for fear of anything they might have picked
up down by those nasty docks." And they were sent
back to bed.

"It was Dido's idea," sobbed Penitence. "She
wanted to go."

"Then it was very weak of you to follow her exam-
ple," snapped Cousin Ann, rustling out of the bedroom and shutting the door sharply behind her.

"Pen, I'm *surprised* at you," Dido said bitterly.
"Don't you know you didn't ought to put the fault on
someone else?"

"But it was *true!* It was *your* idea!"

"Oh, blame it, that ain't the point! Well, don't do
it again, that's all. I'm trying to get you out o' whin-
ing, sneaky ways, Pen, don't you see?"

"Thank you, Dido," Pen said in a small, miserable
voice. "I'll try to remember."

Dido had no chance to lead Pen astray again during the rest of the time they were with Cousin Ann.
She badly wanted to tackle Captain Casket about the
possibility of finding a home for Pen other than with
Aunt Tribulation, and about her own passage to England, but he never came near Cousin Ann's house
again, so busy was he with refitting and reprovision-
ing the ship, and asking all newcomers for news of
the pink whale. Meanwhile the children were kept
under strict supervision, and were only allowed out
for a short walk once a day—to the end of the road
and back.

However, on the ninth day, while Keziah was at a
missionary meeting, Cousin Ann found herself obliged
to lie down with a headache brought on, she said,
by the trampling of children's feet upstairs in the

bedroom. No sooner had she retired than Dido was out of the house like a bullet.

"*You* can stay, Pen, if you're scared to come," she said, "but I wants to see your pa and get things fixed up shipshape."

Pen said she would remain at home in case Cousin Ann needed anything, so Dido flew down the hill to the wharfside. What was her horror, when she reached the berth that had been the *Sarah Casket's*, to find it empty!

"Hey," she said to a boy who was fishing nearby, "where's the ship that was here?"

"Sailed this morning on the early tide."

"She didn't! You're bamming!"

He shrugged. "What d'you think she did, then? Walked away up the hill? The old skipper was raring to go—someone told him that someone said someone else'd seen a pink whale off Gay Head. He was missing his first mate when he sailed, but he said he couldn't wait, so he up anchor and off; guess he's halfway to the Grand Banks b'now."

"Oh, croopus," groaned Dido. She turned and walked wearily back up the steep hill; her legs felt as heavy as lead. "Now we are in the basket! What an old chiseler Cap'n Casket is. I mighta knowed he'd play us a trick like that—sneaking off on the quiet so's Pen couldn't make a fuss, I'll lay! One thing's certain, though—I ain't a-going to stop any longer with Cousin Ann."

Luckily, Cousin Ann was of the same mind. She had had the forethought to collect money for their fares from Captain Casket when he first called, and the very next day they were dispatched to Nantucket, with their new clothes, on the packet *Adelaide*, a small schooner loaded up to her eyebrows with coal, cordwood, and watermelons. Cousin Ann left them in the captain's charge, but it was plain that that harassed man would have little time for them, since part of his cargo was a mother pig and her piglets, which kept escaping and darting about.

"Mind and behave yourselves now" was Cousin Ann's tart parting injunction. "I wrote off last Saturday and told Tribulation to expect you any day, so she'll likely be waiting for you at the Straight Wharf. Give her my remembrances—though why I should send them I don't know, since she was so uncivil as not to call on me when she passed through New Bedford. And I'm sure I wish her joy of you!"

With that, she turned and stumped briskly off up the hill.

"Well," Dido, said, heaving a sigh, "whatever your Auntie Trib's like, Pen, she can't be sharper than your Cousin Ann. So that's one comfort. And at least we can enjoy ourselves on the trip over."

In this she proved wrong, however. The wind was rising, the glass was falling; the captain soon declared that if he'd had the sense to wait another hour or two he'd never have put out. Dido was heartily glad that he had not waited; even being wrecked on the way across to Nantucket was preferable, she thought, to another night with Cousin Ann. But poor Penitence, upset and miserable, retired below and stayed there, wedged as comfortably as Dido could fix her up between a coop of goslings and a barrel of tamarinds.

They were not wrecked, but the rising gale delayed them considerably, and dusk had fallen by the time they rounded Brant Point and were safe in Nantucket

Harbor. Salty, soaked, and shivering, they clambered onto the wharf with their bundles.

"Hey!" the captain called into the gloom, "anyone here from the Casket place?"

Nobody answered. The two children waited for more than half an hour until most of the other passengers, or people unloading goods from the packet, had left.

"Well, it ain't no manner of use standing here all night," Dido said, clenching her teeth to prevent their chattering. "And it ain't half a-going to rain in a minute. What'll us do, Pen? Can we walk to your pa's farm? Is it far?"

"N-nine miles," shivered Pen. "It's much too far to walk with our bundles."

"Had us better put up at an inn?"

"Oh, no! They're sure to be full of horrid, rough sailors."

"Well, I ain't stopping here," Dido said, and led the way into Nantucket town, with Pen following irresolutely. "Maybe we'll see somebody you know if we wander a bit; maybe your Auntie Trib reckoned the packet warn't coming and went shopping or started home again."

They walked along neat brick sidewalks bordered with trees. The bricks were now beginning to shine with rain, the trees were thrashing wildly. Few people were abroad at this hour; the other passengers from the ship seemed all to have melted away into the shadows. Doors and windows in the demure, white clapboard houses were shut and shuttered against the rising storm.

"Bit of a dead-alive hole, ennit," Dido said shivering. "Give me lovely London any day." However, she cheered up somewhat when they reached the wide main street, where a few stores were still open and showing lights.

"I can tell you one thing—I'm crabbish hungry," Dido remarked as they passed a chowder parlor and a heartbreaking smell of food drifted out to them.

"Oh, so am I!"

"Got any money?"

"Why, no," faltered Penitence. "Cousin Ann only gave me the boat tickets."

"Hum," Dido said. She hefted her bundle thoughtfully. Just ahead of them, on the corner of Main and Union streets, was a store with windows still brightly lit up and a sign that said, BRACY AND STARBUCK, SHIPS' OUTFITTERS AND GENERAL SOFT GOODS.

"I'm a-going in here," Dido said, and did so, ignoring Pen's apprehensive squeak. She addressed herself to a man behind the counter.

"Hey, mister, I've got a load of clobber here that I don't want, will you buy it off me?"

To Pen's horror, the man was quite prepared to buy the carefully made dresses and frilly underwear considered suitable by Cousin Ann. "What do I want with 'em?" Dido said. "I'd sooner have a pair of britches any day." She bought herself a red flannel shirt and a pair of denim trousers for one dollar sixty-two cents, and still had two dollars left. "Come on, Pen," she said, "we'll go get us some prog. By the way," she asked the outfitter, "you don't know if there's anybody in town a-waiting for Miss Pen Casket, does you?"

"Little Miss Casket for the Casket farm?" he said. "Why, yes, the old mule's been in every day this week. Guess he's still around; Mr. Hussey at the Grampus

Inn knows not to loose him till the packet's been in an hour."

"Old mule?" said Dido apprehensively. "Who the blazes is the 'old mule?' "

"Why, old Mungo," the storekeeper told her. "Everybody in Nantucket knows Mungo. He's Captain Casket's mule. Old Mrs. Casket—Captain Casket's mother, that was—always used to send him into market with her eggs and farm truck and a list o' groceries she wanted, and Mr. Folger at the Stores would take the eggs and load him up wi' the flour and stuff and send him back. Old Mungo knows the way to Soul's Hill as well as a Christian—he's twenty years old if he's a day. Are you little Miss Casket, then? My, how you have growed!"

Dido didn't wait to chat. "Which way's the Grampus Inn?" she asked. "Come on, Pen. Hurry!" Slipping and stumbling, they ran along the cobbled streets, scaring a number of sheep, who appeared to have come into the town to take shelter, and reached a building with a wildly swinging sign that showed a grampus in full spout. Below the sign was tethered a mule cart; the dejected mule, his coat sleek with rain, seemed trying to keep his head dry by hiding it between his forelegs.

"Is that your pa's cart?" asked Dido.

"I—I'm not sure," Penitence confessed. "I never took much note of the cart."

"Well, is this Mungo?"

"I was always too scared of him to notice what he was like."

"Oy," said Dido, going round to the mule's front end. "Psst, you! Hey! Is your name 'Mungo'?"

The mule made no response, except to give her a

despising glance from one white-rimmed eye, backward, between his legs.

"I'm going in and ask," Dido said.

"Oh, dear, I'm sure you shouldn't go into an inn!"
Pen lamented. "There will be dreadful people. It
isn't ladylike behavior!"

"Oh, *scrape* ladylike behavior!" Dido snapped impatiently. "If *you* want to get soaked and starved, *I*
don't."

She marched into the inn. Having ascertained that
it was indeed Captain Casket's mule and cart standing
outside, she said, "Well, if he's waited for us every
day this week, it won't kill him to wait another
twenty minutes." And, to Pen's fright, she ordered
three bowls of clam chowder. However, the chowder
was so welcome when it came, savory and hot, full of
tender little clams, that Pen at length overcame her
qualms and consented to eat it.

"Who's the third bowl for?" she asked.

"Why, poor old Mungo, o' course," Dido said
reprovingly. "If he's got nine miles to go through the
wet, he ought to have summat to stay his stomach."

"Will he like it?" Pen quavered.

"We'll soon see, won't us? If he don't, I dessay you
can do with a second help."

However, the mule proved quite willing to accept a
helping of chowder, and appeared to improve greatly
in his spirits once he had snuffled it down. The dishes
were returned to the inn. Dido helped Pen into the
cart and wrapped her in a quantity of sheepskins
which she found under the seat; then she untied
Mungo's head, slapped him with the reins, and they
were off.

"Whizzo!" she said, as they rattled through the

dimly lit streets. "This is something like, ain't it? I loves drivin'—if only it didn't rain and blow *quite* so hard. I say, ain't we lucky Mungo knows the way? We'd never find it in this dark."

Pen assented faintly—she had soon left the box and was huddled down in the bottom of the cart, trying to keep herself from slipping about.

In no time they were out of the little town and making their way along a high and exposed sandy track in open country. The wind and rain buffeted them, and it was too dark to see anything except some low-growing shrubs by the roadside. A distant, continuous roar could be heard to their right, and from ahead of them came louder, intermittent booming.

"What's all that row?" Dido asked.

"It's the waves."

"But we've just come from the sea."

"Nantucket's an island, don't forget," Pen sighed drearily. "What you can hear is the breakers on the south and east shores. Oh, how I hate it!"

"Cheer up," Dido said. "Don't you like swimming and paddling? Us'll have some bang-up times when this gale blows over. I used to bathe in the Thames, but this'll be far and away better. I say, I wonder where the old *Sarah's* got to by now, eh? Don't you reckon it was a mean trick of your pa to slope off like that without a word? I'd 'a liked to 'a said goodby to Nate; he was a real fust-class boy. And to old Jenkins. I hope I see them again sometime."

Pen, who for some time past had been growing more and more melancholy, now fairly burst into tears.

"Oh, I don't suppose we'll ever see any of them

again," she sobbed. "They'll probably be wrecked in this gale. And I'll have to spend the rest of my life in this hateful, lonely place with nobody but Aunt T-T-Tribulation. And I hope I die soon, I do! I'd sooner be dead with d-dear Mamma."

"Now, *Pen*," Dido began. But then, instead of scolding, she reached over backward and patted what she could find of Pen in the darkness. She thought her companion's remarks both ungrateful and poor-spirited, but the day had been long and the weather nasty; Pen had some excuse. "I say," she suggested instead, "let's hope that Auntie Trib has a huge big fire blazing and a socking great jog o' red-hot cocoa. Eh?"

Pen made no reply beyond a sniff.

"How about a song to keep ourselves cheerful, one o' Nate's?" And Dido began to sing in a hoarse but tuneful voice:

> "Oh, fierce is the Ocean and wild is the Sound,
>   But the isle of Nantucket is where I am bound—
>   Sweet isle of Nantucket! where the grapes are so
>   red,
>   And the light flashes nightly on Sankaty Head!"

Inspired by this, Mungo the mule actually broke into a canter, and so they went briskly on their way through the storm. Even so, it seemed a long journey, and both of them were thoroughly soaked and stiff with cold by the time that Mungo pricked his ears, accelerated his pace, and made a sudden swerve to the right. In spite of the storm the night was not altogether dark, for there was a full moon now behind the driving wrack of sea mist, and ahead of them a narrow lane could be seen leading uphill from the main highway. From time to time dark forms got up and bundled away off the track as they approached.

"I'm glad we ain't in Hyde Park," Dido remarked. "If we was, these'd be wolves, likely as not; as it is, I s'pose they're some more of those sheep you seem to have such a lot of. Hey, Pen, here's a gate; Croopus, did you ever see sich a peculiar one? Is this your pa's place?"

"I think so," Pen sighed faintly, peering forward in the gloom. "Yes, he put up the gate; it is made of a sperm whale's jawbone. Oh, I am so cold and wet and miserable."

"Ne'mind. In ten minutes you'll be tucked in bed with a warming pan. There's a barn, anyhows; Mungo seems to think he lives here."

In fact, after they had passed the gate, which was like an enormous wishbone, Mungo trotted into the big barn without worrying any further about his human passengers. Penitence was rather impatient when Dido insisted on unharnessing him and giving him a rub with a wisp of hay, "Just in case," she said, "your Auntie Trib don't fancy stepping out into the wet. All right, come on now, bring your traps."

There appeared to be quite a group of farm buildings, set in a hollow of the hillside with a few trees roundabout. Not a light showed anywhere, and it was hard to be sure which was the dwelling house.

"Come on, Pen," Dido urged. "After all, you live here. Show us the way."

"Ye-es," Pen said shivering, "but we were here so little. Mamma took me away on so many visits that we were hardly ever at home."

At last they found what seemed to be a house door and Pen, a sudden memory returning from earlier childhood, stood on tiptoe and discovered a key hanging on a nail.

"Hooroar," Dido said as they stepped inside. "Ain't I glad to get in out o' the wet. Looks as if Auntie Trib musta gone to bed. Know where the candles is kept, Pen?"

"N-no, I forgot," Pen said dolefully. "Oh, isn't it dark and cold!"

Luckily, feeling about, Dido chanced to knock over a candle; when it was restored and lit they saw that they were in a large, old-fashioned kitchen which, given warmth and light, would have been a cheerful enough place. There was a big potbellied stove, black, unlit, and unwelcoming; a brightly colored braided rug; and a dresser covered with dishes. An enormous grandfather clock ticked solemnly against the wall. The place was clean and tidy but silent, empty, and deathly cold.

"Oh," whispered Pen, "what shall we do now?"

"Do? Why, go to bed. Things'll be better in the morning," Dido said stoutly. "Where's the stairs?"

Pen opened a door, disclosing a steep, narrow flight, and Dido went ahead with the candle.

"Hey," she said, checking to let Pen catch up, "look, there's a light under that door at the end o' the passage. Must be your Auntie Trib's room. We'd better go and tell her we've come."

"B-b-but," whispered Pen tremulously, "supposing it *isn't* her?"

She clutched Dido's arm.

"Why, you sapskull! Who else could it be? Come on!"

Dido marched boldly along the passage and rapped on the door.

"Miss Casket?" she called. "It's us—Penitence and Dido, just arrived."

From the room beyond, a voice replied, "And about time, too! Wipe your feet on the mat before you come in."

Even Dido quailed momentarily at the sound of this voice. It was low, harsh, and grating; there was something very forbidding and something strangely familiar about it. Her hand trembled slightly and she spilled a drop of hot wax from the candle, which went out; then, summoning resolution, she pushed open the door and went in.

By the light of one dim candle on the bedside table they could see a woman in the bed, propped against many pillows, regarding them fixedly.

CHAPTER SIX

Aunt Tribulation. Cows and sheep. Green boots in the attic. Aunt Tribulation is hungry. Pen meets a stranger.

"LIGHT ANOTHER CANDLE," ordered the woman in the bed, "and let's have a look at you. Hm," she said to Dido, "you don't favor my side of the family. Must take after that poor sickly Sarah."

"You got it wrong, ma'am," Dido said hastily. "That's Pen there. I'm Dido Twite."

Although she stared at the girls pretty sharply, it was hard for them to see much of Pen's aunt, for she held the bedclothes up to her chin, and had on a nightcap with a wide frill that left most of her face in shadow. They could just make out a gaunt, nut-cracker chin, and a thin nose, so like a ship's rudder that Dido half expected it to move from side to side. A pair of tinted glasses hid Aunt Tribulation's eyes from view. Dido grinned, thinking of the wolf, and subdued an urge to exclaim, "Why, Auntie Trib, what big eyes you have!"

"*You're* a pasty-faced little bag of bones," Aunt Tribulation commented, looking at Pen. "Haven't filled out as you grew, have you? Well, I hope you're both used to hard work, that's all. You'll get no lounging and pampering here." She thumped on the floor with a rubber-shod stick to emphasize her words. "There's all the house chores and the farm work: *I* can't help you, as I've been sick abed ever since I got here; this damp island air turns a body's bones to corkscrews. So you'd best get to bed now; there's the milking to be done in the morning."

"But I can't *milk!*" exclaimed Pen in horror.

"You'll have to learn, then, miss," Aunt Tribulation returned shortly.

"Oh, come on, Pen," Dido muttered. "It's a rusty lookout for the cows, but I s'pose it's got to be done by *somebody*. Where shall we sleep, Aunt Trib?"

"In the chamber at the other end of the passage. Sheets and blankets are in the cedarwood box. Milk the cows at four, take them to pasture, feed the hens and pigs, groom the mule. Light the stove—you'll need to chop some kindling if there's none in the cellar—and the peat's in the peat house—and you can bring me a pot of coffee and a bowl of milk toast at seven. Look sharp now."

Too dazed by the length of this list of tasks to make any protest, the girls retreated and found their room, which was as bleak and clean as at Cousin Ann's, but lacked the washstand, square of oilcloth, and braided rug. Shivering and yawning, they dragged comforters and sheets from the cedar box, made up the bed, and tumbled into it, huddling against one another for warmth.

"I'm that tired I could sleep for a week o' Thursdays," Dido murmured drowsily. "Dear knows how we'll ever wake at four."

Pen fell asleep immediately. But Dido, tired though she was, lay tossing and turning for a long time. Outside the wind sighed over the moors, and a night heron was calling—a harsh, monotonous *quock-quock* that went on and on until Dido, in exasperation, pressed her hands over her ears to shut out the noise.

How'm I ever going to get away from here? she wondered. Aunt Trib's quite as bad as poor old Pen made out, a real, sure-enough Tartar. How'm I going to find someone else to look after Pen or take her part? And why does Auntie Trib's voice sound so blame familiar? Where've I heard it before?

This certainly is a moldy lookout.

Now that Pen was asleep, and it was not necessary to cheer and encourage her, Dido could admit to herself that she, too, felt lonely and miserable. London had never seemed farther away. It was hard to imagine the bright, bustling streets in this dark and windy place.

Her pillow was set with homesick tears before she finally sank into a troubled sleep.

Dido need not have worried about how they were to wake; there were three roosters on the farm whose lusty crowing had the girls roused long before any touch of dawn had crossed the sky. Dressing themselves hastily in warm things—Dido put on the denims and red shirt she had bought—they stumbled downstairs and went out to the byre.

"Chase me if I ever thought I'd have to milk a *cow*," muttered Dido, staring up at them—in the dim light they looked as large as battleships—"but at least there's only three on 'em. Let's start with this yaller one. D'you reckon we could tie her up, somehow,

Pen, while we works on her? Could you hold her tail?"

"Oh, I w-wouldn't *d-dare!*"

Pen was indeed so white and shaking that Dido took pity on her and said, "Here, young 'un, you go feed the hens, you told me you done that with your ma. I'll tackle old Mossface here. And see if you can find some eggs. I'd fancy half a dozen for breakfast; my stomach's a-wrapped round my backbone."

Left alone with the yellow cow, who seemed quite peaceably inclined, the resourceful Dido found a bit of rope and made fast both horns and tail to pegs in the wall, despite doleful bellows of protest. She found a three-legged milking stool and sat down on it. Extracting any milk was another matter, however.

"You needn't trouble to keep kicking the pail over; there ain't a drop in it," Dido snapped when twenty minutes had gone by. She was hot, damp, and tousled, while Buttercup seemed calmly resolved to stand there till judgment day without cooperating.

A cheerful laugh from the doorway made Dido spin round.

"Bless me if ever I saw the like!" the woman who stood there exclaimed. "You'll never get any milk from her that way, child!"

"Doggone it, missus," Dido said, pushing back the hair from her forehead, "how *does* I get milk, then? It'd be easier to squeeze it out of a milestone."

"Here, untie those ropes and I'll show you."

The woman, a good-humored, plump, fresh-faced individual, pulled out a sacking apron she had with her in a basket, put it on, and proceeded to give Dido a lesson in milking.

"You shape at it right well," she said when at last

the three cows were milked. "You'll soon get the hang now you see how it's done. I thought I'd just step over and see was all well; I've been coming here a bit to see to the animals and tend Miss Casket while she was sick. She said her young 'uns was expected this week, but I judged you still might need a bit of help."

"We're mighty obliged to you, missus," Dido said gruffly. "There's a fair deal to learn. Now I'd best go and see if young Pen's got into trouble."

Pen had succeeded in feeding the chickens, but was paralyzed with terror by the hogs; they found her shivering outside their pen, listening to the hungry squeals within.

"They won't hurt you, child," the woman said kindly. "Here, give 'em this bucket of mash." Dido did so. "So you're little Penitence, are you? Bless me, how you have grown since you've been away. Do you mind how we used to come and see you sometimes, and how my boy Nate used to bring over the bantam eggs?"

"Why, you must be Mrs. Pardon!" Pen cried joyfully. "Oh, have you come to help us? You *are* kind!"

"Can't stop long," Mrs. Pardon said cheerfully, "for it's a fair step home, and I've got my old father, Nate's granddad, sick in bed. So we'd best get on. But I can see you're a pair of right smart young 'uns and will soon know your way round. Just turn the cows loose in the bottom pasture, Dido, won't you, and Pen, bring in the eggs."

With Mrs. Pardon's assistance they whirled through the rest of the tasks. She showed them how to light the potbellied stove. "Never heard of burning *earth* afore," grumbled Dido, "and don't it weigh heavy?"

as she stumped up with a bucketful from the outhouse. "That's peat, lovey," Mrs. Pardon told her. "Makes the best smoked bacon from here to Schenectady."

"And don't I wish I had a bit inside me now," Dido sighed, taking out a pail to the log pump, which was so stiff and heavy that both children had to hang on the handle before any water could be obtained.

"This water comes all the way from the White Mountains," Pen remarked. "I remember dear Mamma telling me so."

They staggered indoors with the pail between them.

"Then, why the blazes didn't they take it a bit farther and put a tap inside while they was about it?" Dido said irritably. But things were looking up now; the sun had risen, the stove was crackling finely, and the big kitchen seemed a warm and pleasant place.

"Mercy, I must fly along home, or Pa will wake up and wonder what's happened to me," Mrs. Pardon said, looking at the grandfather clock. "I'll be over tomorrow morning again to give ye a lesson in butter making. You can always come to me if you're in trouble. It's not much more than three miles to my house, just this side of Polpis."

She took off her apron, gave them both a hearty kiss, and hurried away just as a loud thumping on the floor overhead proclaimed that Aunt Tribulation was awake. Pen went up to see what she wanted and was greeted with the words, "Where's my breakfast? You're ten minutes late."

"I—I'm very sorry, Aunt Tribulation."

"Sorry! Sorry's not good enough. Don't forget to cut the crusts off the toast. And scald the coffeepot.

And clear the coffee with eggshells. And when you've brought me my breakfast and washed the dishes and towels, you can scrub the kitchen floor and dust the parlor. Then you'll have to make some bread. And that other girl can hoe the potato field."

"Huh," Dido said when this program was unfolded to her. "Don't she want us to cut down no trees? Or slap a few bricks together and put up a new barn? Anyhows, I'm a-going to have some breakfast before I start on that lot. Here, I'll take up the old girl's prog, Pen. I've fried you some eggs; sit down and get 'em inside you—you look like a bit o' cheesecloth."

Aunt Tribulation received her breakfast tray without enthusiasm. "Wash your face before you come up another time, girl," she said harshly. "And where's my napkin? You should have used the pink china; this is kitchen stuff."

"Lookahere, you ungrateful old cuss," burst out Dido, her patience at an end, "you oughta be thankful I didn't bring it up in a baking pan! Lord bless us, am I glad you ain't *my* Aunt Trib."

She ran out of the room, slamming the door behind her, but was hardly in the kitchen before the thumping overhead began again.

"I'll go," Pen said bravely. "I've had all I want." She gulped the last of her coffee and hurried upstairs. Dido, shoveling down eggs and bacon, heard a long, snarling monologue going on overhead; she could distinguish the tone but not the words. Giving Pen what-for because I sauced her, she thought, and, going to the top of the stairs, she called, "Pen! Pen, come quick. The cows have broke into the tater field."

Pen ran down, looking scared.

"There, there, it was just to fiddle you out o' that old harpy's room," Dido said cheerfully, patting her on the shoulder. "Come on, let's get these crocks washed. Auntie Trib can stew in her own vinegar for a bit. I don't reckon she can be very sick, not if she had the strength to thump the way she's a-doing now."

To Dido's great surprise and relief, Pen proved a handy little creature with the indoor tasks; she had been taught by her mother to wash and bake and cook and polish. She soon took over the making of meals—"which it's as well," Dido admitted, "for I never could abide housework and I don't know a waffle iron from a skillet; eggs and bacon is as far as I go. If I'd 'a had to make the bread, it'd turn out tougher'n old boots. It beats all how you get it to rise so, Pen. You'll have to teach me; one thing, housework ain't so bad when it's just us on our own. In fact, it's quite a lark. Pity the old gal couldn't go back to wherever she came from."

"Oh, Dido," confessed Pen—they were out of earshot of Aunt Tribulation now, sociably hoeing the enormous potato field together—"she frightens me *dreadfully!* Her eyes glare so—at least, I'm sure they do behind her glasses! And her voice is so angry and scolding. Now I know what Mamma meant when she said Aunt Tribulation was a Tartar. I'm sure I shall never get used to her."

"Now, now, Pen," Dido admonished. "Remember as how you're learning to be brave? Every morning when you get up you must say twenty times, 'I am not scared of Auntie Trib.' You'd best start now."

"I am not scared of Auntie Trib," Pen said obediently. But then she broke out, "It's no use, Dido, I *am* scared of her!"

"Well, we'll have to get you out o' the habit," Dido said stoutly. "You watch me. See how I stand up to the old sulphur bottom."

Pen gulped, nodding, but she looked apprehensive.

"Do you remember her now you see her again, Penny?" Dido asked. "Is she like she was when you was small?"

"Just as frightening," Pen said. "But I don't really remember her much. She looks older than I expected. And even crosser than I remembered!"

This is a moldly lookout for me getting back to England, Dido said to herself; how'm I ever going to stiffen up Pen so's she don't mind old Aunt Gruff-and-Grumble? For that's the only chance there seems to be. Who else would come and live out here at the back end o' nowhere?

When the noon hour came they entered the house to the accompaniment of a regular hurricane of thumps from upstairs. Pen ran up to inquire her aunt's wishes and returned trembling and in tears, so fiercely had she been greeted with "Fetch gingerbread and applesauce and look sharp about it, miss! What have you been doing all morning, I'd like to know? Idling and playing and picking flowers, I suppose!"

"Oh, pray, don't scold, Aunt Tribulation—pray, don't. Indeed, indeed, we haven't been idling; we have hoed more than half the potato field."

"Old harridan. I wonder how she knew you'd made some gingerbread?" Dido said. "She must have a nose on her like a bloodhound. There's some apples down cellar, Penny. I saw them when I was getting the kindling for the stove. And there's hams and onions and molasses and bushels of beans, so we shan't starve and nor will old Mortification upstairs."

As Pen hurried to get the apples, Dido, stoking the stove, muttered, "Ill, my eye! If she's so ill, what's her nightcap ribbon doing on the kitchen floor? You've been poking and snooping and spying, you old madam, you, to see whether we did the housework, you horrid old hypocrite!"

When the applesauce was made she took a saucerful up to Aunt Tribulation with the cap ribbon ostentatiously stuck like an ornament at the side of the dish. "I guess this is yours, Auntie Trib," she remarked innocently. "I can't *think* how it come to be lying on the floor downstairs. Acos you haven't been down, have you?"

Aunt Tribulation took this very much amiss. "Impertinent girl! Don't speak to me in that way. Apologize immediately!"

"Why should I?" Dido said reasonably. "You ain't been extra polite to us."

"You shall be shut up in the attic till you learn better manners."

"Tally-ho! I'm agreeable," said Dido. "I can just about do with a nap arter all that hoeing."

"Not now," said Aunt Tribulation, who appeared suddenly to recollect that she had other plans for the girls. "I want you and Penitence to shift the sheep up to the high pasture. And, mind you, count them! Do that as soon as you've washed the dishes. And don't forget to make up the stove. And bring the cows back when you come, and milk them, and shut them up. And skim the cream and make butter."

"Sure that's all?" inquired Dido. "Nothing else as

how you can lay your mind to? Sartin? Tooralooral, then."

"Is you positive there ain't any wolves on Nantucket?" Dido asked Pen as they walked down the sandy lane to the pasture, where the sheep were to be seen grazing.

"No, why? There's nothing but deer and jackrabbits."

"I was only thinking," Dido replied pensively, "as how it would be very convenient if a wolf was to break in and gobble up the old Tartar. Never mind, us'll get her tamed. I'll have her eating out o' your hand before I'm through. Tell you what, Pen, whenever you see her, think to yourself, 'Poor old Aunt Tribulation, I wonder if your rheumaticks is a-troubling you.' Now, how the mischief are we to count these here blame sheep?"

"There's a gate in those railings over there," Pen said. "If you could get behind them and drive them, I could count them as they come through."

"Clever girl, Pen. You've got a right smart head on your shoulders when you doesn't get all of a pucker and a fluster."

Dido ran off across the rough pasture, which was not grass but low-growing scraggy shrubs and bushes. Pen waited by the gate and, conquering a slight tendency to shrink in alarm as the sheep streamed towards her, manfully counted them.

"Two hundred and twenty-three," she said when they were all through and being driven up towards the high pasture. "I wonder if that is the right number?"

"Well, if it ain't, you may lay Auntie Trib will tell

us fast enough. Croopus, don't the wind blow up here, and can't we see a long way!"

"All over the island," Pen said wanly, looking across the rolling, shrubby moorlands to the line of the ocean. On the south shore white, mushrooming clouds of spray from breakers could be seen dimly through a belt of haze.

"What's that white tower to the east?"

"Sankaty Head Lighthouse. There's a forest between us and it," Pen said with a faint glimmer of pride, "but you can't see it. It's called the Hidden Forest. That's uncommon, isn't it?"

"Rummy," agreed Dido. "So's your pa's house. Why's it got a balcony on the roof? And why's it standing on legs?"

"I don't know about the legs. Grandpa Casket built the house. The balcony was for Granny, so she could look out to sea and see if Grandpa's ship was in sight. Mamma didn't like going up there; it made her giddy."

"It's a naffy idea," Dido said. "I'd like to go up. I reckon this is a fust-rate little island, Pen; us can have a fine time here once we've got Auntie Trib pacified."

"Look, isn't that a man coming to call at the house? We'd better go home."

"Race you down the hill," Dido said, and was astonished when Pen nodded, picked up her skirts, and darted away down the sandy track.

But when they reached the house, panting and laughing, nobody seemed to be about. The man had vanished. They ran into the kitchen, and Dido went up to Aunt Tribulation's room.

"Has somebody called here?" she asked, knocking

and entering. There was a sort of flurry from the bed, as Aunt Tribulation huddled down in her pillows. Two spots of crimson showed on her thin cheeks.

"Do not come in until I give you leave, miss!" she croaked.

"Sorry, I'm sure! We was feared you mighta had to get up and answer the door."

"I have done no such thing! Go and milk the cows!"

"Good land, don't be in such a pelter. I'm just a-going," Dido said, injured. Then, recollecting, she added, "Never mind, poor Aunt Trib. Is your rheumaticks very bad?" and shut the door. But in the passage outside she paused, remembering that she had noticed the door next to Aunt Tribulation's opened on an upward flight of stairs. Must lead to that fancy balcony, she thought. I've a good mind to step up—won't take but a moment. She tried the door. Strangely enough, it was locked now, though she was sure it had been open when she noticed it before.

"Why are you loitering out there, girl?" Aunt Tribulation called angrily from her room.

Dido shrugged and ran downstairs.

"D'you want to make the butter, seeing you know how, Dutiful?" she proposed. "I'll fetch in Mossface and make a start on milking."

Penitence agreed gratefully.

"You'll have to face the cows sometime, though," Dido warned. "And I can tell you, they ain't a quarter as fierce as Auntie."

When the milking was done and Dido was helping Pen in the dairy, taking spells with the heavy churn, she asked, "Does that door by Aunt Trib's room lead up to the roof, Penny?"

"Yes, and to the attic."

"Where's the key kept?"

"In the door, mostly," Pen said in surprise. "But there's a spare, because once when I was little I locked myself in there. Oh, I was scared, and so was Mamma!"

"Where's the spare, then?"

"On a hook at the back of the china closet. Why?"

"Just I've a fancy to go up there sometime," Dido replied calmly. She did not add that she was also curious to know what Aunt Tribulation was up to. It seemed clear that while the girls were out she had locked the attic door and taken the key. What could be her reason?

The butter thumped against the side of the churn. "It's come," announced Pen with relief, opening the lid and looking inside.

"That's as well," said Dido, rubbing her biceps. "Another minute and my arms 'ud 'a busted right off at the sockets. What'll us do now?"

"I suppose we're free," Pen said doubtfully. "I'd like to do some lessons. And write my journal and sew my sampler."

"Not on your Oliphant. There's the old gal a-thumping again."

Aunt Tribulation called imperiously for Pen to bring her more gingerbread and applesauce, with a drink of the new milk. "Did you scald the crocks?" she demanded. "And salt the butter? And how many sheep did you count?"

"Two hundred and twenty-three, Aunt Tribulation," Pen quavered.

"One missing! That one must be found, miss."

"Y-y-yes, Aunt!"

"Make haste and set about it, then."

Pen bore up till she was downstairs, but then she burst into tears.

"Oh, I'm so tired! And look, it's nearly dark outside. Do you think we really need go tonight, Dido? I'm sure we'd never find it. And I don't believe I can walk another step."

"Nor you shall," said Dido sturdily. "Be blowed to the old besom. How does she expect us to find one sheep in the dark in umpty miles o' wild country? That's a crazy notion. It'll look after itself till morning, I reckon; we'll find it then. Run along to bed, Pen, while I stoke the stove and lock the back door."

Pen was already half-asleep by the time Dido tiptoed up and snuggled in beside her under the quilted comforters.

"I brought the back and front door keys," she whispered, tucking them under the pillow. "Just so's to be on the safe side. 'Night, Dutiful."

"Goodnight, Dido."

Halfway through the night Dido woke up and lay listening sharply. This ain't half a creaky old house, she thought. Every pine board seemed to have its own separate voice, and when the wind blew it was almost like being on board ship. But no wind was blowing now, and yet a board had creaked. She was sure it was a board. Outside she could hear a night heron croaking on the moors, but this was a different sound, quite close at hand. Burglars? Dido slid a hand under the pillow and satisfied herself that both keys were still there. Pen slept peacefully. The creak was not repeated and, after a while, Dido, too, drifted back into sleep and dreamed that she was asking Aunt Tribulation to lend her the fare to England, while Pen weepingly begged her not to go, and Aunt Tribulation made no reply except to shake her red wattles, wink a black, beady eye, and croak, "Certainly not! Certainly not! Get up, you lazy girl! Cock-a-doodle-doo!"

"Wake up, Pen, it's morning."

"Oh, no, it can't be!" moaned Pen. "I could sleep for hours longer."

"Never mind. At least we shan't have to light the stove this morning. I can just about do with some bacon and coffee."

They dressed in the warm kitchen. While Dido was brushing Pen's long hair, Pen said, "That's odd. I thought we left the window fastened. Look, it's only pushed to."

Dido considered the window in frowning silence for a moment before going out to the byre. But she only said, "Oh well, lucky nobody noticed it and got in."

Mrs. Pardon appeared again to help them with the morning tasks and was amazed to find that they had managed to make the butter themselves.

"Why, you're a reg'lar pair of young farmers!" she declared. "I'd best teach ye how to make cheese, then, and soap. I've brought ye some goodies—I know young 'uns always like candy. And a mess o' pooquaws in case your auntie fancies a bit o' fish. Is she any better today?"

"We haven't seen her yet this morning."

"She was in rare, brisk spirits last night," Pen and Dido said together.

"She is a rare, brisk 'un, isn't she, your auntie? I was surprised when I seed her—she's not a bit like Cap'n Casket."

"Hadn't you seen her before, then?" Dido said, surprised.

"No, lovey. She's never lived in Nantucket since she was a gal, you see. She went off to live with her grandmother in Vine Rapids."

Dido pondered over this, while the animals were tended and the cheese-making went forward. Then, she thought to herself, there's nothing to prove that this lady is Aunt Tribulation at all. Pen doesn't really remember her. But if she isn't Aunt Tribulation, who is she?

Dido milked, while Mrs. Pardon showed Pen how to cook the pooquaws. Then, after they had breakfasted, and while Aunt Tribulation was graciously accepting the delicacy, inspired by a sudden idea, Dido found the spare attic key and ran softly upstairs. She slipped the key into the keyhole—it fitted, the door opened—and she tiptoed on up the next flight. She found herself in a huge room with a sloping roof and low dormer windows. It stretched the length of the house and was filled with all sorts of odds and ends— old trunks, old boots, boxes, bales of sacking, flour bags, two stuffed birds under a glass cover, some wooden stub-toe skates, an old fowling gun, and so forth. Dido looked around sharply. She did not quite know what she was searching for, but almost at once she found it: faint, sandy footprints on the floor.

Those weren't made long ago, Dido said to herself. If they had been, they'd soon 'a dried up and blowed away.

A ship's ladder and a trapdoor led out onto the roof; looking down from the widows'-walk balcony, Dido saw Mrs. Pardon hurry away down the track towards Polpis. I'd best be getting back to work, she thought, before the old gal finds I'm up here, and she closed the trapdoor and tiptoed down the ladder. At its foot she stopped short, riveted by the sight of something that she had missed on her first, hasty survey of the attic. Behind one of the chests, as if they had been hurriedly thrust out of sight, was a bundle of ladies' clothes: bonnet, gloves, a black silk dress, and a cloak of gray twill. On top of the bundle was a pair of bottle-green boots.

Dido tiptoed over and inspected these. They had white stains on them.

Salt water, she said to herself. *Those* haven't been here long.

I'd best get out o' here.

After giving another quick, darting look round the attic, she slipped down the stairs and softly closed and locked the door behind her. None too soon, it seemed; she could hear terrified wails coming from Aunt Tribulation's room.

"Dido said I might go to bed!" Penitence was saying through her tears. "Dido said we'd never find it in the dark. And, indeed, Aunt Tribulation, we were dreadfully tired. Dido said th-that looking at night-time was a crazy notion."

"She did, did she? She shall be punished for that. And you, miss, had better go out now, and I don't wish to see you again until the sheep is found! I am going to make myself obeyed from now on, do you understand?" Aunt Tribulation rapped on the floor with her stick.

Frowning, Dido walked into the room.

"So, girl!" Aunt Tribulation addressed her fiercely. "You countermand my instructions, do you?"

"Yes," Dido agreed. "They were downright addlepated. And you didn't oughta shout at Pen that way; you'll scare her into historics. Pen," she added, more in sorrow than anger, "haven't I told you about not putting the blame on someone else? Stick up for yourself, girl!"

Pen gave her a miserable glance.

"Still, we mustn't be too hard on the old gal," Dido added, with a sudden seraphic smile at Aunt Tribulation. "When she shouts at you, Pen, remember her rheumaticks is hurting her cruel bad."

Plainly, Aunt Tribulation did not quite know how to deal with this.

"Penitence!" she snapped. "Be off!"

Pen hesitated, then ran from the room.

"As for *you*," Aunt Tribulation went on, "you can miss your dinner. Go out, finish hoeing the potato field, then do the cornfield, and don't come back till it's finished."

"Blister your potato field," Dido replied calmly. "I'm a-going to help Pen find that sheep. And if I miss my dinner, so will you, acos there won't be no one to bring it up to you."

With which parting shot she ran downstairs to the kitchen. Pen had already started down the track. Dido quickly put up a bundle of food—bread, butter, cheese, a handful of dates, and the candy sticks Mrs. Pardon had brought with her. "Miss my dinner be blowed," she thought; then she ran out after Pen, who could be seen trudging miserably along about half a mile in front. Dido waved and called unavailingly—Pen was too far away to hear, and the wind was blowing the wrong way—and hurried in pursuit. I mustn't be hard on Pen, she thought as she ran; it's bad enough for the poor little creep to be bawled out by Aunt Tartar without me bearing on her too. But she does try a body's patience at times. Weak, like her da.

At last she caught up with Pen. "Hey-o!" she shouted. "Look, I brought us a picnic. If we're to spend a day on the moors, we might as well enjoy ourselves and make it an outing."

Penitence looked affrighted. "But she said you were to miss you dinner! I heard her, all the way down the stairs."

"Look, Pen," Dido said patiently. "Whose vittles is these? Your pa's, ain't they? He asked me to stay with you, didn't he? *He* didn't say I was to miss no dinners. And who done the work? Who fed the pigs and milked the cow and made the bread? You and I done it; Auntie Trib never done a hand's turn. So she've got no call to order us about."

Pen seemed so astonished and alarmed at these revolutionary ideas that Dido left her to digest them in peace while they searched for the missing sheep. There were plenty of others to be seen grazing the rough pasture as they went farther afield, but not one with the red "C," which was Captain Casket's mark. At last, when they were about halfway to Polpis and the sun was high in the sky, Dido suggested that they should rest and eat.

"I wonder if you couldn't stay with Mrs. Pardon?" she suggested, as they sat on a bank munching their bread and cheese.

Pen's face lit up.

"Oh, do you suppose I could? She is so kind and nice. But perhaps she is too busy with her sick father."

"Glad of another pair of hands, I dessay," Dido

said. "After all, you're handy about the house, Pen. But I s'pose we'd have to get your pa's permission or Auntie Trib'd never let you go. And the mischief is, how to find him if he's off again chasing his everlasting pink whale. Why don't you set your fist to writing to your pa?"

"Do you think a letter would change his mind, Dido? I'll write to him just as soon as I can," said Penitence.

"Oh, look, Pen! I do believe that there's a sheep with a red mark. Look, by the bushes. Quick, let's go arter him. Brrr! though; ain't it turned cold all of a sudden."

While they were eating, the children had not noticed that a fine, white sea mist had come creeping over the island. Just as they started after the wandering sheep the mist caught up with and engulfed them.

"Hey, where are you, Pen?" Dido called anxiously.

"Here! I'm here!"

"Blame it, it's like walking through porridge! Where in thunderation is your voice coming from? Stand still, till I find you," Dido said, feeling her way forward, but Pen suddenly shouted excitedly, "Oh, I see it, I see the sheep! I believe I can catch it, too!"

There came the sound of running footsteps, which faded into the distance, then a disappointed cry, "Oh, drat!"

Missed it, diagnosed Dido. Seconds later a damp, dew-spangled sheep bolted past her, nearly knocking her down, and disappeared into the dimness before she could grab it.

Blazes, Dido thought. Now I've lost 'em both, Pen

and the sheep. Which'd I better go after? Pen, I reckon. The sheep can look after itself.

"Penitence!" she called lustily. "Du-oo-tiful! Penitence! Where are you?"

No answer—only a plaintive, faraway bleat. Not *you*, woollyknob, Dido thought crossly. She floundered on into the smoky whiteness, tripping over wet, tangling shrubs, getting caught in thornbushes and low-growing holly, stumbling into holes and out of them again.

What a blame-awful country, she thought. Why can't they have some decent grass, 'stead of all this dratted scrubbage that tears your shins to ribbons? Thank goodness I've got britches on; poor old Pen in her thin, white stockings must be getting scritched to pieces.

"PEN! Where are you?"

This time there was no answer at all.

Doggedly, Dido went on hunting and calling. She must have covered acres of ground in the course of the next two or three hours, but never had so much as a glimpse of either Pen or the sheep. At last she struck a track which led uphill. Dark was falling by now. Dispirited, weary, and very worried about Pen, she turned along it. Maybe I'll come to a house or a farm, she thought, where I can ask somebody to give me a hand hunting. At this rate the poor little brat stands a chance of being out all night, and that'd just about *do* for Pen; she'd be seeing ghosts and boggarts for the rest of her life.

She hurried along the track, which sloped more and more steeply uphill and suddenly brought her out into a familiar barnyard. Why, curse it, Dido thought angrily, I'm *home*. What's the good o' that?

No hopes Auntie Trib will give a hand. I'd best turn right round and go back the other way to Mrs. Pardon's.

She was just turning wearily down the dusky track when a lantern light showed in the barn door.

"Dido!" called Pen's eager voice. "Is that you?"

"Penny!" Dido exclaimed joyfully. "You're back, then!"

"Yes, and, what do you think? I found the sheep again! Wasn't that a bit of luck? And, Dido, I have had such a curious adventure. Listen—"

"You found the sheep? You brought it back all on your own?" Dido was amazed. "I'd never 'a thought you had it in you, Pen! How ever did you manage to fetch it along? Where is it now?"

"In the barn. I led it," Pen said.

"How, for gracious' sakes?"

"Well," Pen said rather shyly, "I thought, how would Dido set about it? And, as I hadn't got a rope, I took off my stockings and tied them together. It was the sheep that found the way home really, not me. But I was dreadfully worried about where you'd got to, Dido. I'm ever so glad to see you."

"Well, us'd better turn to and do the evening jobs while there's still a glim of daylight," Dido said. "You can tell me about your adventure when we're indoors making supper, Pen."

They made haste with their tasks. Both were tired, wet, and hungry—though Dido grinned to herself as she thought how much hungrier Aunt Tribulation would be.

"Done the fowls? Good. That's the lot, then," she said to Pen as they met at the back door.

"Oh, Dido," breathed Pen fearfully, "there's a light in the kitchen. Do you suppose—?"

"Ssh!" Dido laid a milky finger on her lips and opened the kitchen door.

The kitchen was warm and bright but had lost some of its cheerful atmosphere. For Aunt Tribulation, fully dressed, was sitting in the rocking chair by the stove. She was no less formidable up than she had been in bed; although she had taken off her tinted glasses, the gray eyes they had concealed were cold and singularly unwelcoming. She wore a brown-and-white checked gingham dress and a brown shawl; an enormous brown brooch, with enough hair in it to stuff a pincushion, fastened her white fichu. Her gray hair was strained back into a tight knot behind her head. She looked hungry.

"We found the sheep, Aunt Tribulation!" Pen announced proudly, after a momentary check in the doorway.

"So I should hope! You've taken long enough about it. Is the milking done? Then hurry up and make my supper."

"Pen must change first," Dido said firmly. "Her dress is sopping and she's got no stockings on."

"Make haste, then. And, pray, why were the larder and cellar doors locked, and what have you done with the keys?"

"Oh, dear, did you want them?" Dido exclaimed innocently, drawing the keys out of her breeches pocket. "I locked the doors acos we found the kitchen window open this morning, and I was feared that burglars or wild animals might get in and steal our vittles or frighten you, Auntie Trib! O' course I never thought you'd be coming down for summat; I thought you was much to ill. I *am* sorry! Did you get peckish, then?"

Aunt Tribulation did not answer, but looked daggers while Dido, pretending not to notice, made up the stove and started frying bacon.

"Pen'll do some pancakes when she comes down. She's a dab at pancakes. And she set a pot o' beans a-baking in the oven this morning; what a shame you never thought to look in there, isn't it, Auntie Trib. You coulda been eating baked beans all this time."

Supper was taken in baleful silence, and as soon as the children had washed up the dishes they escaped to bed, Dido almost bursting with suppressed laughter.

"Now tell me your adventures, Dutiful," she said when they were snug under the quilt and the candle blown out.

"It was the strangest thing! After we lost each other I hunted for you, and I ran towards where I thought you had been standing, but I must have gone astray, for I ran on and on, a long way, and suddenly I found myself among high trees."

"Trees? Why, there ain't but bushes and bits of scrub for miles."

"I must have been in the Hidden Forest, you see," Pen explained. "It seemed so mysterious in the mist! When I called to you (as I had been doing on and off all the time) my voice echoed back so boomingly that I was afraid and dared not do it anymore. I became confused in the wood and, trying to return the way I had come, went on, I think, in quite the wrong direction. Then all of a sudden I found myself up against a strange kind of barrier."

"A fence, like?"

"No, not a fence, nor yet a wall. . . . It was about as high as my head and very thick, and round like a great iron pipe; yes, like an iron pipe as big as a great tree trunk."

"That's rum," Dido said. "What held it up, then?"

"It was mounted all along its length—and it was *very* long; I never saw either end—on pairs of cartwheels."

"Sounds as if maybe someone gets their water through it," Dido suggested.

"But there are no farms anywhere near the Hidden Forest! It is a solitary place."

"Well, I dunno what to make of it," Dido said, yawning. "You never knew it was there afore?"

"No, never. But that's not the end of the story."

"No? Hurry up, then, Dutiful. My eyes is closing in spite of themselves."

"I thought I would feel my way along the pipe, and so get out of the wood. But I had not gone very far when I bumped into a man."

"What sort o' man? What was he doing?"

"Oh, Dido, he was strange! He was tapping on the pipe with a hammer. He gave a great start when I bumped into him. I would have screamed, but that *he* seemed even more frightened! I said I was lost, and which way to Soul's Hill? And he said, 'Whisper,' laying his finger on his lip and looking all round, and then he pointed which way I should go and led me to the edge of the wood. Then he whispered something, and it took me *such* a long time to make out what he was asking—he spoke in such a strange, foreign way! At last I realized that it was *boots* he wanted—he showed me his feet in thin, foreign-looking shoes, all wet and torn and muddy. So I promised I would have

a look at the farm—there might be an old pair of
Papa's sea boots, and was that all he wanted? And he
said—I *think*—that he had a great longing for something sweet—could I bring him any cakes or sugar or
jam? To keep out the cold and damp. He said he
would wait by the fork in the track every night from
seven till nine."

"Was he a beggar?"

"No, indeed, I am sure he was not! For he gave me
money to pay for the boots—three English gold coins."

"*English* coins?" Dido was suddenly wide awake.
"How d'you know they were English?"

"Because there is a picture of a king and the words
'*Carolus II Rex Br.*'"

"Good cats alive!" Dido said. "An old guinea
piece! There's still quite a lot on 'em about. My pa
used to get them for playing on his hoboy. D'you
think the man was English, Pen?"

"He certainly was not American. But he didn't
speak like you—his language was very queer. He was
a sad-looking man with a face like a monkey, and big
ears, and nearly bald. He said not to tell anyone that
I had seen him, and if I came with the boots I was to
croak like a night heron."

"Night heron? What's that? One of those birds that
go on yakking all the perishing night?"

"Yes," Pen said. "I think that was what he meant.
And he said how glad he was that he would soon be
back in Europe."

"*Did* he?" Dido was more and more interested. If
this man is really going back to Europe soon, she
thought, and if I could make friends with him, and if
I could get Pen fixed up to stay with Mrs. Par-

don. . . . Who can the man be? Oh, is there a chance that I could go with him as far as London?

"We must look him out a pair o' boots tomorrow, Pen," she said. "I don't mind taking 'em to him if you're scared to go back. There's a deal of old boots up in the attic."

And one pair of salt-stained, bottle-green ones that ought not to be there, she remembered, just before she went to sleep. Was it not probable that Aunt Tribulation and the veiled stowaway of the *Sarah Casket* were one and the same person?

CHAPTER SEVEN

Aunt Tribulation gets up. Second trip to the attic. Dido's in the well. Return of Captain Casket. Trip to the forest. The conspirators. The gun.

AUNT TRIBULATION had evidently decided that it was easier to keep an eye on the girls if she got up, for the next day they were disconcerted to find her established in the kitchen when they came in from the morning's milking.

"This room is disgracefully dirty and untidy," she said grimly. "After breakfast you, miss," she said to Penitence, "may bestir yourself to give it a good scrub and cleanout. *You*," this to Dido, "take Mungo and the cart down to the peat swamp to fetch a load of peat."

"I'll help Penny first, and then she can come with me," promptly replied Dido, who had no intention of leaving Pen to fend for herself for so long with Aunt Tribulation.

"You'll do as I say, and don't argue about it!"

Dido did not argue about it, but when Aunt Tribulation retired after breakfast, leaving the girls to wash up, she fetched a bucket of water and began to scrub the floor.

"I'll do that Dido—you'd better go!" whispered Penitence, alarmed.

"And leave you on your own? Not likely! Hurry, and we'll be done afore she comes down."

Aunt Tribulation, when she did come down, was very angry. "How dare you disobey me, insolent girl!" she thundered, looking about for her stick. But Dido, accustomed to self-preservation in the hubbub of the London alleys, had prudently removed the stick, chopped it up, and burned it in the stove. Aunt Tribulation boxed her ears instead, and told her to go and sit on the whale's jawbone for two hours, reciting, "I must not be a naughty, insubordinate girl."

This Dido did not at all mind doing. True, the jawbone was not very comfortable to sit on, but it was close at hand, so that she would wave cheerfully and shout encouragement whenever Pen's duties took her across the barnyard, and it made a change from work.

After an hour or so, Dido had an idea. "Psst! Penny!" she called, as Pen came out with a basin of wrung-out cheesecloths. "Come this way a minute?"

"What is it?" Pen hung her cloths on the clothesline, starting at the end nearest Dido, but keeping an anxious eye on the kitchen door.

"That span'l dog of your auntie's—the one that bit you—"

"It didn't bite me," the truthful Penitence interjected. "I was afraid that it might."

"What was it called?"

"Toto." Pen recalled the horrid creature with a shudder. "I am so *glad* she didn't bring it with her this time."

"Probably died years ago. But never mind that,"
Dido said. "Don't you think as how it would be polite
and sociable to ask arter Toto's health? Might put the
old gal in a better humor."

"Do you think so?" Pen said doubtfully.

"Well—try, Penny, and see! Just say, 'Aunt Tribulation, how's Toto?' and see what she says."

Slightly puzzled, Pen obeyed. Dido was unable to
hear the conversation, which took place in the
kitchen, but the result was most satisfactory. Pen
came flying out, looking scared, to report in a whisper, "She was as cross as two sticks! First, she didn't
seem to remember Toto at all, and when I reminded
her, she told me to get along out and hoe the corn
patch and not bother her with silly chatter!"

At this moment Aunt Tribulation put her head out
of the kitchen door and called sharply, "Hurry up,
miss! Don't dawdle there! And *you* go, too," she
added with a fierce scowl at Dido, "so that I can have
a bit of peace and quiet! Work hard, mind! I shall be
out presently to see how much you have done."

"Tooralooral," said Dido, sliding down the whale's
jawbone. "Come on, Penny."

"What are you giggling about?" the mystified Penitence inquired as they carried their hoes towards the
corn patch.

"Just that I believe it ain't going to be too hard to
manage the old bag o' bones." But Dido did not con-
fide her growing conviction that their taskmistress was
not the real Aunt Tribulation at all, as her ignorance
about Toto seemed to show.

It was not, however, always so easy to circumvent
Aunt Tribulation, now she had decided to come
downstairs and take charge of the household. Indeed,

as Dido said, it was hard to believe she had ever been ill at all, so active and vigilant was she now in pursuit of keeping the children hard at work. Reprimands for real or fancied faults fell thick and fast, since she made no allowance for inexperience, and expected all tasks to be carried out with perfection, both indoors and out.

"What does she take us for, perishing slaves?" grumbled Dido.

Even without her stick, Aunt Tribulation found no difficulty in devising punishments. Dido, who constantly incurred her displeasure, was frequently deprived of meals, shut in the grandfather clock, and had her head rapped with a thimble. Pen succored Dido when she could, bringing her tidbits, opening the clock to whisper condolences, and rubbing the bruised head with wintergreen ointment.

"As well as learning you to stand up to Aunt Tribulation, Pen, we've someway got to make her *humble,* so she's real sorry for her nasty nature and won't never bother you no more," Dido observed one morning when they were out taking salt to the sheep.

"Do you think that would *ever* be possible? I'd much sooner go and live with Mrs. Pardon," sighed Penitence.

"Yes, but we can't fix that till we've heard from your pa. Aunt Trib certainly wouldn't want to lose a handy cook-parlormaid-farmhand-dairymaid like you, Pen. Have you written the letter to your pa yet?"

"Yes, I have it in my chemise pocket."

"Now, the mischief is, how're we going to get it to Nantucket to post it? No use to give it to old Mungo and ask *him* to take it to the mail office."

Market days had come and gone, but Aunt Tribulation had sternly vetoed any idea that Dido or Pen might go in with the farm produce and do some shopping. Mungo, as usual, was sent on his own with a written list of groceries needed, which the owner of the main store would check and supply.

"If we could give the boots to your monkey-faced friend, *he* might post the letter for us," Dido presently reflected. "The trouble is how to wheedle Aunt Trib out o' the house so's I can slip up to the attic and grab a pair. She never stirs except just across the dairy."

"I could tell her one of the sheep was sick and ask her to come up to the pasture."

"She wouldn't care," said Dido, who privately suspected that Aunt Tribulation knew little more about farming than the girls themselves. "No, I have it, Penny. You must pretend you think I've fallen down the well. She wouldn't like that; no water, for one thing, and who'd do the milking? She'd come out to help you grapple for me with a rope, and I could nip round to the back and climb up the willow tree and in our window."

"But if she found out?" breathed Pen in horror.

"We could say you made a mistake. I'll drop my red shirt down, so's it looks like me down there," said Dido, to whom Mrs. Pardon had recently given some old shirts of Nate's, cotton, with NEW BEDFORD FLOUR MILLS stenciled across the back, which were more comfortable in the hot weather. "Pity we couldn't drop Auntie Trib herself down."

In pursuit of this plan, Dido contrived that evening to smuggle out her red shirt hidden in a pile of cheesecloths, and dangle it down the well on a loop of thread until it caught on a projection about thirty feet below. The weather favored them; it was misty again, and dusk was falling. Dido beckoned to Pen, who was in the henhouse, and whispered, "Now, *screech!*"

"Oh!" faltered Pen, "I don't believe I can!"

"Consarn it, Pen, you'd screech fast enough if a wild bull was rushing at you! Let on that one is!"

Pen gave a faint wail.

"Louder than that!" hissed Dido. "Here, I'll do it!" She let out a fearful scream and then quickly slipped away round the corner of the house. The back door flew open and she heard Aunt Tribulation's voice.

"What's the matter?"

"Oh, Aunt T-Tribulation," Pen stammered, "I'm— I'm afraid Dido's in the well."

"Blimey, *she'd* never get to Drury Lane," Dido groaned to herself as she rapidly shinnied up the willow tree. "I never heard such a rabbity bit of acting." She scrambled in at their chamber window and pulled the spare attic key out of her pocket.

In a moment she had darted up to the attic and seized the largest and least worn pair of sea boots; then, on a sudden thought, she tiptoed to the bundle of clothes behind the chest, pulled out the bonnet, and looked inside. It bore a London dressmaker's label and a name: "Letitia M. Slighcarp." So did the cloak. Dido did not dare wait to examine the rest of the clothes; she fled silently down the stairs again, relocked the door, and was out and dropping from the willow tree all in the space of half a dozen heartbeats. She could still hear voices and splashings from the direction of the well, so she thrust the boots into a clump of fern, strolled nonchalantly round the corner, and remarked, "Hilloo? Dropped summat in the water?"

It was well she arrived when she did, for Aunt Tribulation had tied a rope round Pen, who had a perfectly ashen face and was shaking like a leaf, and was apparently on the point of lowering her to the assistance of her companion.

"You abominable girl! Where have you been?" Aunt Tribulation exclaimed, dashing at Dido and boxing her ears.

"Down the orchard, hanging up the cheesecloths. Why, whatever's the matter?"

"Didn't you hear us shouting? Penitence thought you were in the well."

"No, did she?" Dido replied, and burst out laughing. "You *are* a one, Pen! You musta seen my shirt; that blew down when I was taking it to hang out. What a sell!" And she began to sing:

> *"Oh, what a sell,*
> *Dido's in the well.*
> *Who'll save her bacon?*
> *Auntie Tribulation!"*

Aunt Tribulation, perfectly enraged, exclaimed, "So you thought you'd make a fool of me, did you? Oh, you wicked little hussies. You shall have nothing but bread and water till the end of the week!" And she flew at Pen, who was the nearer, and shook her till she whimpered, "It was Dido's idea, Aunt Tribulation, not mine! P-p-please stop! It was Dido's idea!"

"Oh-oh," Dido said to herself. "Here we go again. Now we *shall* be in the suds."

But just at this critical moment an interruption occurred.

By now it was thick dusk and they could see only a few yards. Sounds, however, carried clearly in the mist, and they suddenly became aware of voices and footsteps approaching up the lane.

"Someone's coming!" breathed Penitence.

Aunt Tribulation turned her head sharply, heard the voices, and hissed, "Go indoors, you girls! Make haste!"

Astonished, the girls did as they were bid, but went no farther than the deep porch. They were too curious to know who the visitors might be, for no callers had come to the farm since their arrival. Was Aunt Tribulation expecting somebody?

A voice—a boy's voice—said, "Here we are, I b'lieve. Ain't this the Casket place?" and then, apparently seeing Aunt Tribulation, "Evening, ma'am. Would you be Miss Casket?"

"Yes, I am," she snapped, "and I don't allow tramps and beggars on this land, so be off with you both!"

"But ma'am—" the boy began to protest, and then Pen gasped as a man's voice said slowly and wonderingly, "Why, isn't this Soul's Hill? We're home! However did we come to be here?"

"Be off!" Aunt Tribulation repeated.

"But, ma'am! He's your brother! He's Cap'n Casket. Don't you *know* him?" the boy blurted out, and at the same moment Pen cried, *"Papa!* It's Papa come home!" and Dido shouted, "Nate! Nate Pardon! What in mercy's name are you doing here?"

Both girls rushed forward joyfully, but checked a little as they came in view of Captain Casket. He

looked thin and dazed, older than when they had
seen him last; in a few weeks his hair seemed to have
become a great deal grayer. But he smiled dreamily at
Pen and said, "Ah, Daughter, I am glad to see thee
well."

"Nate, what's happened?" Dido said quickly in a
low tone. "It's not the ship—the *Sarah Casket*—?"

"We don't know," Nate replied in the same tone.
"Let's get him indoors, shall we, before I tell you
about it. He's still not himself."

"Come in where it's warm and dry, Papa," said Pen
protectively, and took Captain Casket's hand to lead
him in. He looked about him, still with the same bewildered expression, and said, "So thee is living at
home now, Penitence? I am glad of that. But who is
this?" pointing to Dido.

"Why, Dido Twite, Papa. Don't you remember
her?"

"Perhaps," he said, passing a hand across his brow.
"I am tired. I become confused. Then who is looking
after thee?"

"Papa, don't you remember Aunt Tribulation?
Here she is! She has been—has been looking after us."

"Ah, yes, Sister Tribulation. She said she would
come," he murmured.

At this moment Aunt Tribulation, who had remained in the rear while these exchanges were going
on, stepped forward, firmly took Captain Casket's
other arm, and said, "Well, Brother! Fancy seeing you
home so soon! Deceived by the mist, and never thinking but that you were several thousand miles off, I almost took you for a tramp! This is a surprise, to be
sure! What has become of your ship? Not a wreck, I
trust?"

She seemed less than pleased at seeing her brother; indeed, thought Dido, she seemed decidedly put out.

Captain Casket looked at her in his wondering manner and murmured, "Can it really be Sister Tribulation?"

"Of course, it is I, Brother! Who else should it be?" she exclaimed impatiently, leading him in.

"Thee has aged—thee has aged amazingly." He sat down in the rocker, shaking his head.

"We're none of us getting any younger!" snapped Aunt Tribulation.

"He is still a bit wandering in his wits, ma'am," Nate explained in a low voice. "What he's been through fair shook him up."

"What happened?" Penitence inquired anxiously.

"It was the pink whale, you see."

Nate glanced towards the captain, who seemed to have gone off into a dream, rocking back and forth, soothed by his chair's familiar creak and the homely things about him.

"We sighted her about ten days out o' New Bedford," Nate went on, "and, my stars, did she lead us a dance! Round and round about, first north, then south. In the end we was nearer Nantucket than when we first started. At last we came right close to her, closer'n we'd ever been before; lots of the men hadn't rightly believed in her till then, but there she was, sure enough, just about like a great big strawberry ice. Well, Cap'n Casket, he says, 'No man goes after her but me,' he says, and he wouldn't let any o' the harpooners go in the boats. Just the one boat was lowered. He said I could go, with some of the men, because I had an eye for detail and a gift for language, and would be able to record the scene."

"Well, and so? What happened?"

"She acted most uncommon," Nate said. "*I* never see a whale carry on so. Soon's she laid eyes on Cap'n Casket she commenced finning and fluking and bellowing, she breached clean out of the water, she whistled, she dove down and broke up agin, she brung to dead ahead of us, facing us with her noddle end, and kind of *smiled* at the cap'n, then she lobtailed with her flukes as if—as if she was wagging her tail like a pup, she rolled and she rounded, she thrashed and tossed her head like a colt, she acted just about like a crazy porpoise. By and by she settled and started in swimming to and forth under the dory, rubbing her hump on the keel, and that busted the boat right in half."

"She didn't know her own strength," murmured Captain Casket as if to himself. "She meant no harm. It was only in play."

"What happened then?" breathed Dido, round-eyed.

"I don't know what happened to the other men in the boat," Nate said. "We was all tossed out a considerable way. I just about hope they got picked up by the ship. I was swimming near Cap'n Casket in the water when we was both heaved up as if a volcano had busted out under us, and blest if it wasn't old Rosie hoisting us up on her back! And you'll never believe it, but she started to run then, and she never stopped till she brung to and dumped us off Sankaty Beach. Then she sounded, and we never saw her no more. So we waded ashore and walked here. I reckon the cap'n had best be put to bed, ma'am."

Indeed, Pen, who found this tale almost too frightening to contemplate, had already busied herself with heating some bricks in the oven for the captain's bed, and warming one of his spare nightshirts before the fire.

"Oh, Papa," she paused by him to say, "I am so *thankful* you were spared."

He patted her head absently. "Is that thee, Daughter? What is thee doing on board? I thought I left thee in New Bedford."

"He must certainly go to bed," pronounced Aunt Tribulation.

"I'll be off home, ma'am, now I've seen him safe here," Nate said. "My ma'll sure be surprised to see me."

"But have a bite to eat first—have a hot drink!" Dido exclaimed. "Try some o' Pen's herb tea and her pumpkin pie—it's fust-rate. And you haven't told us what happened to the ship. Did they see you thrown into the sea and picked up by the pink 'un?"

"I guess not," Nate said. "There was considerable fog come up. Like as not if the other men gets picked up, they'll reckon me and Cap'n Casket musta been drowned."

"Well, you ain't—that's the main thing," Dido said. "Oh, Nate, your bird! Poor Mr. Jenkins! Was he with you in the boat?"

"No, no, chick, he'll be all right," Nate said, laughing. "Reckon Uncle 'Lije'll look after him for me till they puts back into port."

Aunt Tribulation now bustled Captain Casket upstairs, while Pen started heating a milk posset for him. "Oh, Dido!" she whispered, "I'm so happy Papa has come home! For Aunt Tribulation will hardly—will hardly like to be so unkind to us while he is here."

Dido nodded sympathetically. In fact, she was by no means so easy in her mind about the situation. For a moment, at first, she had hoped that, if Aunt Tribulation really was an impostor, she would be exposed by Captain Casket's failure to recognize her as his sister, but it was soon plain that he was too wandering in his wits for this to be likely. And if he continued so, Dido feared that he would have small effect on Aunt Tribulation's sharp and bullying ways. And what would become of his promise to secure Dido a passage to England? In any case, she could hardly go off and leave Pen while matters were in such a train. Her heart sank. There seemed less and less chance of her ever reaching London again.

Nate wiped his mouth and rose. "Thanks for the pie; it was real good," he said. "I'll be on my way."

"Oh, Nate," Pen said earnestly, "I'm so *grateful* to you for bringing Papa safe home!"

It was the first time she had ever plucked up courage to address him directly, and Dido gave her an approving look. Nate smiled down at her.

"That's all right, little 'un," he answered awkwardly. "Hope he's soon better."

"I'll come out with you," Dido said. "I hain't shut up the cows yet." And she muttered to Pen, "I'll take the boots along to you-know-who while I'm out. If *she* asks where I am, say the yaller cow got loose and I'm chasing her. Needn't bother about getting your letter posted now, that's one thing."

"Nor we need!" Pen said, recollecting. "Oh, Dido, take the poor man this sassafras candy too!" And she gave Dido some brightly colored sticks that Mrs. Pardon had brought that morning.

"I'm coming a piece of the way with you," Dido ex-

plained to Nate when they were outside. "I've an errand in the forest. Lucky there's a moon behind the
clouds."

The sandy track showed up white ahead of them.

"The forest?" Nate said, surprised. "That's a
mighty queer place to have an errand."

"Oh, Nate!" Dido exclaimed. "*Everything's* queer
altogether! I'm right-down glad to see you, I don't
mind saying. I reckon there's some regular havey-
cavey business going on."

"What sort o' business?"

"Well," Dido said, "I don't reckon as how things
can be wuss'n they are now, so I might as well tell
you the whole story."

Which she proceeded to do, omitting nothing: the
veiled lady on the ship, Mr. Slighcarp and the boots,
the torn-up letter, the night departure in New Bedford Harbor, the mysterious visitor at the farm who
had so inexplicably vanished, the footprints in the attic, the sounds in the night and the open window,
and the green boots and clothes marked "Letitia
Slighcarp."

"Whatever do you make of it all?" she asked.

"Seems as if old Slighcarp's muxed up in it somehow, dunnit?" Nate said. "He never sailed this trip,
so he must be ashore somewhere."

"Yes, I know," Dido said. "A chap in New Bedford
told me as how Cap'n Casket had sailed without his
fust mate. D'you suppose old Slighcarp's lurking
somewhere in these parts?"

"Guess so," Nate said perplexedly. "But why?"

"Shall I tell you what I think, Nate?"

"Yes, what?"

"I think Aunt Trib isn't the real Aunt Tribulation at all."

"Who is she, then?"

"I think she's the Letitia M. Slighcarp who left the duds up in the attic. I s'pose she's old foxy-face's wife, or his sister, or his ma, and he's skulking roundabout, coming to see her when we're out o' the way."

Nate considered. "Reckon you're right," he said at length. "But then, what's happened to the real Aunt Tribulation?"

"I dunno. Oh, Nate, d'you think they could have *murdered* her?"

"Easy, now," said Nate. "More likely she jist changed her mind and decided not to come to Nantucket, after all."

"Yes, maybe," agreed Dido, relieved. "And that's why she never called on Cousin Ann in New Bedford; Cousin Ann was in a fair tweak about it. Oh, yes, Nate, o' course that's it, that's why old Foxy Slighcarp tore up the letter at Galapagos! It musta been another one from the real Auntie Trib saying she couldn't go to Nantucket arter all, and he read it—it had come open, remember?—and fixed to put old Mortification in her place." Dido suddenly chuckled. "No wonder the old gal wasn't over-and-above pleased to see Cap'n Casket come home! No wonder she thought he was a tramp at fust! She'd never met him before. Mr. Slighcarp musta brought her here while we was still in New Bedford with Cousin Ann. But what's the point o' lodging her here? Someone'd be sure to rumble her in the end."

"It surely is a puzzle," Nate said. "But wait a minute, wait! Old Slighcarp had to leave England and skedaddle abroad in a hurry because he'd been plotting against the King, and the militia was after him. Maybe it's the same with her. Maybe she had to skip quick, and when he saw this chance he grabbed it."

"Aha!" said Dido. "D'you reckon she got taken on board the *Sarah Casket* at the same time as you picked me up?"

"Could be," said Nate. "We was several days off the English coast. That would explain why old man Slighcarp was so powerful keen to follow the pink whale round thataway, if he knew Miss Slighcarp wanted taking off."

"Of course! That must be it! But what'll us do now?"

"Well," Nate said, "I s'pose the best thing would be to get holt o' the real Aunt Tribulation. Tell you what—I'll ask my ma to write to her at Vine Rapids. Meantime, best lay low."

"Oh, Nate, that's a good plan."

"But you still haven't told me why you're going to the forest."

"That's summat quite different. Pen met a rummy little cove there, camping beside a big iron pipe, and he asked her to get him some boots and candy. He gave her three English guineas and said he was soon going back to Europe. I was curious about him; I reckoned I'd go along to see was there a chance of my getting a berth on his ship. Reckon this changes things, though; I can't lope off till it's settled about Auntie Trib." She gave a deep sigh.

"Funny that there's *two* lots of skulking strangers camped out in Nantucket," Nate said. "Or d'you think this one's anyhow connected with old Slighcarp? Else what the blazes can he be doing here?"

"Pen said he was scared stiff o' summat. He told her to whisper and to croak like a night heron when she came to meet him." Dido chuckled at the thought of Pen trying to imitate a night heron. "Maybe he's scared of old Slighcarp?"

"I dunno what to make of it," said Nate. "Hadn't I better stay with you while you give him the boots? Sounds a mite chancy to me."

"Done," said Dido promptly. "Maybe you'll be able to smoke his lay. But you better glide along kind of cagey in case he sheers off when he sees there's two of us."

"Where was you meeting him?"

"At the fork in the track."

"That's only half a mile now." Nate sank his voice to a whisper. "You keep on the track and I'll slide alongside in the scrub."

Dido nodded. He slipped into shelter and she went on at a good pace, but walking as silently as she could on the sandy path.

When she reached the fork, easily visible in the cloud-filtered moonlight, she squatted down by a wild-plum thicket, cupped her hands round her mouth, and let out a gentle croak. This was answered almost at once, and somebody moved out of the thicket. It was not possible to see him very clearly, but Dido recognized the small, bald man of Pen's description.

"Is it little kindgirl?" he whispered. "You boots with?"

"Yus," Dido whispered back. "I brung 'em."

"But you are unsame child!" Alarm and suspicion could be heard in his voice.

"I'm her friend, guvnor," Dido reassured him. "She

was a-seeing to her pa and couldn't come out. Sorry we ain't been here sooner—it warn't so easy to get aholt o' the boots. This here's candy."

"Ah, miracle, nobleness! All the time is only to eat fish, fish, fish! You are a heaven-sentness," he whispered. His language was both guttural and hissing; Dido found it very hard to follow. He was already sitting in a bayberry bush and pulling on the boots with little grunts of satisfaction. "*Gumskruttz!* Forvandel! Zey are of a fittingness! I am all obligation."

He fervently kissed Dido's hand, much to her astonishment, dropped his old shoes in the bush, then, whispering "Plotslakk! Momentness—I bring you—" vanished back into the thicket. Almost at once he reappeared, thrust a prickly, wriggling bundle into Dido's arms, tried to kiss her hand again, thought better of it, said urgently, "Each nat will be a bringness. Hommens. For you. If you bring kaken?"

"Kaken?"

"Pankaken. Appelskaken. Siggerkaken."

"Cakes," Dido guessed. "I'll try," she whispered.

"Is good, noblechild! Wunderboots! Blisscandy! I say good nat."

Before she could stop him, he faded back into the bush as if something had startled him. "Hey!" Dido whispered as loud as she dared. "Mister! Come back!"

But he was gone.

After a few moments Nate rose soundlessly out of the shrubs where he had been lying, almost at Dido's feet.

"Well," she whispered. "What did you make of *that* lot? And what in tarnation's he given me?"

"Lobsters." Nate identified the wriggling mass. "Big 'uns too. He was a rum job, wasn't he?"

"One thing's for certain." Dido was disappointed. "He ain't English. Pen was right. Dear knows what peg-legged lingo that was he spoke."

"I'd sure like to know what he's doing in Nantucket," Nate muttered. "Up to no good, I bet. I've a good mind to nip into the forest and scout around."

"Oh, yes, Nate, let's!"

"Not you, chick. It wants smart scoutwork. One's enough."

"I can snibble along jist as quiet as you!" Dido said, hurt. They argued about it in whispers; Dido was so insistent on coming that, in the end, Nate was obliged to give way.

Proceeding with the utmost caution, they crept towards the forest. The ground began to slope steeply downhill, and presently they were in the shelter of the trees, where, as it was much darker, they had to go forward very slowly, one step at a time.

Nate, who was a couple of paces ahead, suddenly let out a stifled grunt.

"What's up?" breathed Dido, coming alongside.

"Nearly busted my nose on the tarnal thing. Must be the pipe," he muttered. "We'd best follow it."

They turned at right angles and stole along beside the pipe, slowly and carefully, Nate still in the lead. Presently he paused. A faint light showed ahead and voices could be heard. Dido moved up as close behind Nate as she could and peered past him. The lobsters, which she still carried, nipped the hand that Nate had put out to check her, and he let out a hiss of protest.

"Mind, stoopid!"

"Sorry!"

They could dimly see a small log hut. A fire was

burning in front of it, and three or four men were gathered round talking in low voices.

"Where's the old professor gone?" one of them said.

"Oh, he likes to mooch about the wood on his own in the evening. He's everlastingly on the lookout for the night-crowned black heron or some sich foolishness. He's all right, don't fret about him, he won't go far."

"I'd rather he stayed in camp, just the same."

With a start, Dido recognized this voice as Mr. Slighcarp's. She gave Nate's shin a gentle kick. He nodded.

"When's the *Dark Diamond* due?" another voice asked.

"Any day now."

"Thank the Lord. I can just about do with a decent smoke. I'm *cheesed-off* with smoking peat in my pipe and eating shellfish. Will the ship wait and take us off at the same time's she leaves the powder and shot?"

"Depends on how the professor makes out. If he can finish before she gets here, fine; we can blast off and then clear out."

"What about your sister?"

"Take her too, o' course."

"But ain't she *wanted* over there?"

"But don't you see, things'll be different in England by the time we get back," Mr. Slighcarp said impatiently.

"But supposin' old Breadno makes a mistake? We don't want to go sailing over and put our heads into a hanknoose and end up on Tyburn!"

"We'll sail to Hanover first, dunderhead! The news will have reached them by then."

"Aye, that would be best," the other voice agreed gloomily. "I does so *long* to get my chops round a bit o' British bubble-and-squeak."

"Bubble-and-squeak! It'll be roast goose and champagne when you get it, cully!"

"I'm going to look for the professor," Mr. Slighcarp said uneasily. He rose to his feet.

At this moment one of the lobsters Dido carried, which had been squirming more and more vigorously, escaped from her grip and fell into a bush. She grabbed it.

"Hark! What was that?" Mr. Slighcarp said, turning sharply.

"It's only the professor, guvnor. Here he comes."

By a great piece of good fortune, the man to whom Dido had given the boots—apparently the "professor" referred to—stepped into the clearing at this moment.

"Hey, there, Professor Breadno, see some good nightbirds?"

"We're all just about nightbirds, if you ask me," yawned one of the men. "I'm going to turn in."

Dido kicked at Nate's shin again and began to step delicately backward. She was apprehensive of another accident with the lobsters. Nate waited for a few more minutes before following, but presently joined her on the edge of the forest.

"Did you hear any more?" she breathed.

"Nope. They were asking the prof where he got his boots, and he said he found 'em in a bog."

"I wonder if they'll believe him. What a parcel of peevy coves, eh? Regular mill-kens. They're Hanoverians, that's plain enough."

"I still can't make out what they're at," Nate said, as they hurried silently back to the path. "What the mischief are they doing in Nantucket? We ain't got none o' your fancy kings over here; a plain president's good enough for us."

"It's plumb mysterious," Dido agreed. "Tell you what, though, I'll take the little professor cove some cakes—if I can slip past old Mortification—and try to get a bit more out o' him. Supposin' I can make out what he means."

"I'm glad I came back home," Nate said. "I think it's downright rusty the way these lowdown skallywags make themselves at home in our island, and whatever deviltry they're plotting, I think they ought to be rousted out someway."

"I'm agreeable," Dido said. "Specially if Aunt Tribulation's one of 'em. I allus thought she was a no-good. What d'you think we ought to do, Nate?"

"I'll think, and let you know. I'll stay home for a piece, anyhow. Guess if Grandpa's sick my ma'll be quite glad to have me minding the sheep and helping with the chores. I won't try to get another ship till the *Sarah Casket* comes back. I'd sooner ship with Cap'n Casket when he's better. I'm used to him."

"If he gets better," Dido said doubtfully. "If he don't, I reckon I'm stuck here for life."

"Well, there's plenty wuss places than Nantucket you could be stuck in."

As they were by now a good way from the forest, Nate burst into song:

> *"I'll tend to my lambkins in pasture asd grove,*
> *A shepherd I'll be and daylong will I rove;*
> *In the isle of Nantucket I'll finish my days*
> *A-following my sheep and a-watching them*
> *graze."*

"What'll your ma do if you start spouting poetry at home?" Dido teased him.

"I'll have to wait and spout it to you and Pen," Nate said cheerfully. "There's the lights of Soul's Hill. Can you find your way now? Goodnight. See you soon."

"I do wonder what those 'scallions is up to," Dido speculated.

"Well, whatever it is, it's bad business. I'll tell you one thing, chick."

"What's that?"

"That there pipe of Pen's ain't no pipe but a *gun*—and it's the longest gun I ever laid eyes on!"

"Croopus!" said Dido. "That's why the ship's coming with powder and shot. But who're they going to shoot, d'you reckon?"

"Search me. But whoever it is, they've gotter be stopped."

CHAPTER EIGHT

Captain Casket's illness. Dido sees the doctor. The professor in the bog. An abominable plot. Aunt Tribulation overhears.

To DIDO'S SURPRISE and concern, there were still lights burning in the farm as she approached. Surely it was long past the usual hour for bedtime? Did this mean that Aunt Tribulation had seen through Pen's story of the straying yellow cow and was waiting up to conduct an inquiry?

When Dido walked into the kitchen, however, she saw at once that the unusual wakefulness was not on her account. The stove was roaring, a large black kettle steamed. Pen was anxiously heating a poultice, while Aunt Tribulation, with a grim expression, aired blankets, nightcaps, and chest protectors before the fire.

"Oh, Dido!" Pen exclaimed. "Papa is dreadfully unwell; he is in a fever! I have tried him with everything—balsam and cordial and rheumatic pills—but none of them did him any good. He tosses and turns so, and throws off the bedclothes; he seems to think he is in a boat."

"Did you find the cow, miss?" Aunt Tribulation snapped at Dido.

"She's in the barn," Dido replied. "D'you think we should get a doctor?" she said to Pen.

"Oh, I do! Would you go for one, Dido?"

"A doctor will hardly thank you for fetching him out at this hour," Aunt Tribulation remarked sourly. "Here, miss, take these things up to your father; *I'm* going to bed. I've done all that can be expected in my delicate state of health."

"Isn't she perfectly hateful," Pen whispered when Aunt Tribulation had departed. "She doesn't seem to care a *bit* about poor Papa. As for her 'delicate state of health,' I don't believe there was ever a thing wrong with her." Pen was distractedly looking through the store cupboard in search of more remedies. "What's in this jar? Can you read the label, Dido? It's dear Mamma's tiniest writing. I can't make it out." Impatiently she rubbed the tears from her eyes. "Oh, Dido, supposing Papa were to *die*?"

"We shan't suppose any such nonsense," Dido said firmly. "Huckleberries in gin, this is. Smells like stingo stuff. Try them on him, Penny; see if he likes 'em."

They hurried upstairs with the warm clothes and the poultice, the pot of huckleberries, and a stone jar full of boiling water for the captain's feet.

It was very difficult to get him wrapped up and poulticed. As Pen had said, he kept throwing himself about, crying, "Towno! Towno! Alow from aloft! I'm all beset, bring to! Give it to her, she's pitching. Her spiracle's under. . . . Stern all, we're stove!"

He sprang up in bed, and the poultice flew across the room.

"Never mind the dratted poultice," Dido said at last in exasperation. "It's all cold and dusty by now, anyways. Here, you hold his hands a moment while I try to slip some o' these huckleberries down him. Hold tight!"

Pen held on manfully. "Papa! Don't you know me?" she pleaded. "It's Penitence!"

"Thar she blows!" shouted Captain Casket. But as he kept his mouth open to prolong the bellow, Dido neatly popped in a spoonful of the huckleberries. The captain immediately shut his mouth. He swallowed. A surprised expression came over his face.

"Quick! Another spoonful!" whispered Pen.

When Dido raised the spoon again he opened his mouth eagerly, and she was able to feed him the rest of the potful without difficulty. He murmured to himself, "Truly it has been a wonderful summer for the fruit, wonderful! We must all—"

His eyelids fluttered down and he suddenly fell back on the pillow, fast asleep.

"*That's* a mussy," Dido said. "Now let's snug him up warm, and then as soon as it's light, Pen, I'll go for the doctor. D'you know his name?"

"I *think* it's Doctor Mayhew," Pen said doubtfully. "Anyone in Nantucket town would be able to tell you."

They wedged the captain about with hot bottles and laid several comforters on him. Pen sat down by him, anxiously holding his hand. Since her father had come home, needing her help, Pen was a changed creature. She seemed to have thrown aside her needless fears and become quite practical and self-reliant.

Dido busied herself in tidying the room and remov-

ing the unwanted poultice. It did not seem worth trying to sleep, as there wanted but an hour to daylight;
instead she milked the cows and harnessed Mungo. As
she went indoors again a pink streak was showing in
the eastern sky. She tiptoed up to the captain's room
and found that he was beginning to stir and mutter
again. He half opened his eyes and stared dreamily at
the window.

"Why," he whispered, "it's a little whale calf, no
more than a sucker, washed up on Quidnet Beach!
The pretty little thing, it's as pink as a wild rose! I
won't tell my father, it's too pretty to hurt. I'll put it
back in the sea. . . . There you are, little pink
'un, swim away back to your mother . . ."

Dido had found another jar of huckleberries. She
silently passed it to Pen, who managed to feed a few
of them to the captain, and he went back to sleep.
Dido then gave Pen a brief account of her meeting
with the little man in the wood, to which Pen listened somewhat distractedly; most of her attention
was on her father.

"I'm off, now, Dutiful," Dido whispered. "I'll be as
quick as I can."

Pen nodded.

Dido ran down, jumped into the waiting cart,
shook up the reins, and stared Mungo at a rattling
pace towards Nantucket. One thing, she thought—it's
nice to get into town for a bit, even if it ain't London. I hope Auntie Trib don't give poor Pen the
runaround while I'm gone; likely she'll sleep a good
while yet, as she was up so late.

The day was a fine one and her spirits rose. Dawn
had flooded the upland commons with ruddy light
and crimsoned the distant line of the sea. Old Rosie

would look just the thing out there now, Dido said to herself. For the first time she recalled Nate's strange tale of how the pink whale had seemed to welcome Captain Casket. A rummy business altogether, Dido reflected.

Mungo was suffering from several days' lack of exercise and bolted along so fast that when they descended the gentle incline into Nantucket town it was still quite early. Not many people were about in the cobbled streets. Dido bore right towards the waterfront and left Mungo tethered to a post in Whale Street while she asked her way on foot.

"Old Doc Mayhew?" said a fisherman on the wharf. "He lives on Orange Street. That ain't but a few minutes from here."

The doctor lived up on the hill in a handsome white house, Quaker style, with a fanlight and three windows on each floor. Dido banged loudly on the door and told the housekeeper that Doctor Mayhew was wanted urgently.

"He ain't taken but a mouthful of breakfast. Could you wait ten minutes?"

"Oh, well, I guess Cap'n Casket won't die in that time," Dido agreed. She was dying for some breakfast herself and strolled back, looking for a baker's shop, but was soon startled by a familiar voice, calling in the next street:

"In the spring of the year when the blood is
    too thick.
There is nothing so good as a sassafras stick!
Who'll buy my stick candy
So nice and so dandy?

Pickled limes, jelly doughnuts, come snap 'em
　up quick!"

"Nate!" Dido exclaimed, and ran into Main Street,
where she found Nate making his way slowly along in
a small pony cart laden with trays of delicacies, pre-
sumably made by Mrs. Pardon.

"Hallo, chick!" he said when he saw her, and then
filled his lungs again and shouted:

"I've several different kinds
Of pickled tamarinds!
Try my pickled bananas, walk up, take you pick!
Try my licorice roots, worth a dollar a lick!"

A number of housewives came to their doors and
bought his wares, which included doughnuts, biscuits,
and waffles.

　　"Try my
　　lemony
　　wintergreen
　　sassafras
　　peppermint
　　superfine candy, a penny a stick!"

Children came running for the dazzlingly colored
candy sticks.
He called:

"Popcorn and peanuts and pecans and popovers,
Wintergreen wafers and hermits and jumbles,
Gingersnaps, crullers, marshmallows and turnovers.
Sample a cookie and see how it crumbles!"

Dido bought some popovers and found them delicious.

"Nate, have you thought what we oughta do yet?" she asked, when there was a momentary lull in the stream of customers.

"Yes," he said, glancing about. "I've thought. We must tell the mayor. Likely he won't be so keen to have a mess o' Hanoverian English plotting on his island."

"That sounds like sense. What's the mayor's name, where does he live?"

"It's old Doc Mayhew; he lives on Orange Street."

"Why," Dido exclaimed, "I'm just a-going to fetch him to come and see Cap'n Casket, who's got the raving fevers. Couldn't be more handy. I'll tell him the whole tale as we drive home."

"Oh, that's bully. I'll get this lot sold off and come along to your place later; Ma said as how I was to help you and Pen with the chores when I'd finished selling."

Dido nodded, and as the doctor might be supposed to have finished his breakfast by now, she unhitched Mungo and drove back to Orange Street, where she found him waiting.

Doctor Mayhew was a fine-looking old gentleman with white hair and a frill of white whiskers all round his red face, so that he looked rather like an ox-eyed daisy. He wore a green coat with brass buttons as big as half-dollars, and a snowy-white ruffled shirt.

"Hallo!" he said at sight of Dido. "*You*'re a young 'un I've never laid eyes on before. Didn't bring *you* into the world! Living out at the Casket place, are ye?"

"That's it," Dido agreed. "I'm staying there, keeping young Pen Casket company till she's gotten used to her auntie Tribulation."

"Tribulation Casket? Has *she* come back to live on the island? Why, I haven't set eyes on her since she was a young thing of fifteen."

"Oh." Dido was disappointed. "Guess you'll find she's changed a bit, then."

"Lively young gal she used to be," the doctor said reminiscently. "Always one for a song or a bit of dancing or horseback riding."

"Croopus," said Dido. "She ain't like that now. Doc Mayhew, can I ask you summat?"

"Why, certainly, my child! How can I help you?"

"Well, you see, it's like this, Doc. There's a whole passel of Hanoverian plotters on Nantucket, and we think Miss Casket is one of 'em."

"Hanoverians?" Doctor Mayhew seemed somewhat bewildered.

"Yes, sir. English Hanoverians. They're all a-plotting against the English King."

Doctor Mayhew laughed heartily. "Why, child, what an imagination you have!"

"It's true," Dido said indignantly. "I ain't bamming you!"

"Why, child, even if you were right, what harm could they do the English King over here? This sounds like pure fancifulness to me."

"They've got a gun," Dido said stubbornly. "They're all a-camping in the Hidden Forest—except for Miss Casket, that is—and they've got a mighty great gun about a mile long."

"Oh, no, my child. I have heard of those men. They are scientists, and that is not a gun but a telescope; quite a natural mistake to make. I believe they are ornithologists, studying our bird life; somebody said they wished to see a black-crowned night heron. English ornithologists, that's all they are."

"Orny thologists be blowed!" said Dido. "Ornery jailbirds is what they are, and they're here to do some piece of sculduggery; we heard 'em plotting it the other night in the wood; then they'll go back to England in their ship the *Dark Diamond*."

"That's all right, then," said Doctor Mayhew comfortably. "And good riddance to 'em, whether jailbirds or bird fanciers. We've got no call to worry our heads about a pack of foreign English, even if they do put in a bit o' plotting in the evenings after they've finished bird watching for the day. This is a free country, dearie. And we keep ourselves to ourselves on Nantucket. We've no truck with such highfalutin' nonsense as kings; even the President don't bother us much. 'Live and let live' is our motto. And as for Miss Tribulation getting mixed up in such doings, that sounds like moonshine to me."

"Maybe it does," Dido said crossly, "but it's true just the same. You see, she *ain't* Miss Tribulation. She's only pretending to be her."

"Who the blazes," said Doctor Mayhew, "would want to *pretend* to be Miss Tribulation Casket? You've been reading too many fairy tales—that's what's the matter with you! Now, you tell me what ails Cap'n Casket?"

Deciding that Nate might be a better hand at convincing the doctor, Dido abandoned the subject of the Hanoverians and described Captain Casket's symptoms and strange, delirious remarks. Doctor Mayhew was very interested in the tale of the pink whale.

"Is that so?" he kept saying. "That's mighty interesting. And why shouldn't there be a pink whale, now? There's a-plenty pink fish, pink pearls, pink shells, pink seaweed in the ocean—why not a pink whale?"

"And why did she carry on so when she saw Cap'n Casket?"

"Oh, that's simple enough. Guess she was the little pink whale calf he put back in the sea when he was a boy; he told me that tale once: he found her beached and dragged her back in. *And,* of course, whales, being warm-blooded, warm-hearted, long-lived critters—I've heerd of 'em living to a century or more— she'd naturally remember him kindly. They're kin to porpoise, ye know, and porpoises are right sympathetic to the human race."

"Oh, I see," Dido said. "Kind of old childhood pals, like? Well, we'll be properly in the basket if he wants her to sit by his bed and hold his hand. Let's hope he's a bit better, time we get back."

Captain Casket did not seem to be much better, though, when they arrived at Soul's Hill. He was wild and feverish, rolled about in his bed, and kept throwing imaginary harpoons at unseen whales.

"He needs a dose of poppy syrup," Doctor Mayhew said. "That'll give him some rest."

He administered a draught. Immediately Captain Casket fell back as if he had been pole-axed and began snoring loudly.

"That'll fix him for a good few hours," Doctor Mayhew said with satisfaction. "Powerful strong it is, the way I mix it. Here," he said to Pen, "I'll leave ye the bottle, but don't give him any more unless I'm delayed getting back to ye and he seems worse. Now, why don't I drive your mule on to Polpis, where I want to see old Mr. Pardon, and bring him back tomorrow. That'll save you an extra trip to Nantucket."

Aunt Tribulation came into the room.

"Well, Tribulation," the doctor said, "I'd not have known ye, but I suppose we're all getting a bit long in the tooth. Remember when I pushed you in the creek and you were so mad at me?"

"Yes, I do," said Aunt Tribulation frostily. "And it's not a thing to boast about. It was not the act of a gentleman!"

Doctor Mayhew laughed very heartily at this and took his leave, pinching Pen's cheek. As soon as the door closed behind him, Aunt Tribulation turned fiercely on Dido.

"What do you mean, miss, by going to the Hidden Forest and begging lobsters off the English scientists? Who gave you leave to do such a thing?"

Oh, dear, thought Dido. She met the eyes of Pen, who looked anguished.

"Yes, indeed, I got the whole story out of Penitence," rasped Aunt Tribulation. "And I won't have such behavior! You are not to pester those men, who are very busy botanists studying the plant life of the island, and have no time to waste on prying, spying children, who ought to be at home anyway, tending to their tasks. For that, miss, you shall be shut in the clock, and shall have no dinner or supper."

She suddenly pounced on Dido, who, sleepy and off-guard after the eventful night and long drive, was no match for her and was soon thrust into the grand-father clock. Aunt Tribulation slammed and locked the door.

"Oh, well," Dido thought, yawning, "it'll be a chance to catch up on my sleep." She curled herself up as comfortable as possible, with her head well below the swing of the pendulum, and prepared for a nap. Then, to her astonishment, she heard Pen crying indignantly, like a lamb at bay, "Aunt Tribulation, you are unjust! It is wrong to put Dido in the clock! You should not do so! If anybody is put in there it should be me."

"It should be *I*, Penitence," Aunt Tribulation corrected coldly.

"Hear, hear!" shouted Dido from the clock.

"Silence, disobedient girl! As for you, Penitence, I cannot shut you in, since you are needed to look after your father. You may give me the milk posset you had prepared for him, since he will not need it at present—no, heat it up first—then polish the parlor floor."

Pen's spurt of courage seemed to have died; there was silence for some time; then she could be heard saying in a subdued manner, "Here is the posset, Aunt Tribulation."

Dido went peacefully to sleep, lulled by the clock's solemn tick-tock.

She was not suffered to sleep for very long, however; the door of the clock suddenly opened, letting in unwelcome daylight, and Pen's excited voice whispered, "Dido, Dido, you may come out!"

"Glorious me," Dido murmured, only half-awake. "What've you done with Auntie Gruff? Dropped her down the well? You coulda knocked me down with a feather, Pen, when I heard you speaking up to her so fierce!"

"Oh, but I have done something much, much worse now!" whispered Pen, looking quite scared at her own daring. "I put some of the poppy syrup in her milk posset and she has gone sound asleep on the parlor sofa."

"Pen! You never!"

"Truly! Come and see!"

Dido climbed stiffly out of the clock and saw that it was so. Aunt Tribulation was in a deep sleep.

"Dido, I am truly sorry that she found out you had been to the forest," Pen went on hurriedly. "I could not bear for you to be thinking that I told on you. Indeed, it was not like that."

"Never mind, young 'un," said Dido. "I could see it musta been an accident."

"It was the lobsters, you see; we forgot all about them, and when she woke up, there they were clambering about the barnyard. And she said, 'Where did they come from,' and I—I am not clever at inventing things on the spur of the moment—and I said, 'We had them from a man in exchange for some boots.' And she seemed to know about the man and the boots, so it all came out."

"You could have said they was from Mrs. Pardon."

"That would have been a downright falsehood."

"Oh," said Dido. "Yus, I suppose it would. Eh, well, no use chinwagging over spilt chowder. How's your pa, Pen?"

"Still fast asleep. But I think he looks better."

They sat with Captain Casket through the afternoon, but he continued to sleep peacefully and never stirred. During this time Dido took the opportunity of giving Pen a complete account of what had happened in the forest and the conclusions that she and Nate had reached. But she did not mention their suspicions of Aunt Tribulation; she thought the news that Miss Casket might be wanted by the English police would prove too much for Pen's new-found courage.

At last, when dusk was beginning to fall, Dido said, "Maybe us'd better get the jobs done while Cap'n Casket's still quiet."

Pen agreed that it would be safe to leave her father for a while.

As they were feeding the pigs Pen thought she heard cries from the bottom pasture.

"Dido, quick!" she cried, looking over the fence. "There's somebody in trouble down there on the bog!"

At the foot of the hill was a small cranberry bog half grown over with bushes and straggly trees. They could hear the cries for help clearly now, and see somebody floundering about among the crimson hummocks.

"I'll go," Dido said, grabbing a long-handled, wooden hayrake. "You'd best stay here, Pen, in case your pa wakes."

She bolted down the hill, calling, "Hold on, I'm a-coming!"

When she reached the edge of the bog she saw that the person in distress was the little Professor Breadno. He was mired up to his knees, completely stuck; his eyes were bulging with fright, and his ears stood out like wings.

"Well you *are* a clodpole, ain't you?" Dido said. "How ever did you come to get into sich a pickle?"

"Is hoping seeing bird, seeing Nat-herrn," he explained humbly.

Dido crawled out with caution onto a fairly safe-looking hummock and extended the rake in his direction. He was just able to grab it.

"That's the dandy! Hold on between the spikes!" Dido said, demonstrating. "Now I'm a-going to pull, so when I say 'heave,' you shove off like an old bullfrog. Ready? *Heave!*"

She threw herself back, pulling until every muscle in her skinny frame seemed about to snap. The professor came out of the mud a reluctant six inches and fell forward onto his knees.

"Keep a-going, don't stop now, don't sink!" shouted Dido, throwing herself back again. "Heave some more, come on, put a bit o' gumption into it. Don't pull *me* in!"

She dragged him slowly through the mud.

"If you've lost those boots I shan't half give you whatfor," she added. "We had trouble enough over them already." He was so muddy that it was impossible to tell whether he had them on or not.

"Skrek verlige öfalt!" he exclaimed, looking at himself dolefully, and then, politely, said to Dido, "Is a much nick of time, treasurechild!"

"Yes, thanks, but don't kiss my hand again," she said, retreating with haste. "You better come up and get under the pump. It's lucky Auntie Trib's out for the count." She beckoned him and he followed trustfully, dripping mud and ooze at every step.

"Mercy!" exclaimed Pen at sight of him. "I'll put on a kettle."

"Pump first," Dido said grimly. "It's *us* as'll have to

scrub the kitchen floor if he walks on it in that state.
Make him some o' your herb tea, Penny."

The poor little man submitted meekly to being
pumped over; "I sank you; sank you!" he kept repeating piteously.

"I should just about think you nearly did *sink* me!
Guess you're clean enough now, you can go into the
kitchen." She gestured towards the door, where Pen
had an old suit of Captain Casket's ready. It was far
too big for the professor, and they had to kilt it up
here and there with lengths of string.

He drank the herb tea with loud expressions of ap-
preciation; they gathered it was something he had not
expected to find outside his native land.

"Hjavallherbteegot! Wundernice! Gratefulness!"

"That's all right," Dido said. "Have some gingerbread. Now, we don't want to get you into trouble
with your friends, but we do want you to tell us
about that gun o' yours, Professor."

"Gun?"

"Cannon. Pistol. Bang, bang!"

"Aha, königsbang! Is soon blowing up London."

"*What?*"

"Is will be monstershoot, grosseboom, across—"

He looked about the room and saw an old, silvery
globe of the world on one of the dresser shelves. With
a finger he traced a course on it from the island of
Nantucket up over Nova Scotia across the North Atlantic to London. "Is shooting up palast—Sint Jims
Palast, not?"

"Shooting right across the Atlantic? Blowing up St.
James's Palace. Is that what he means, Pen?"

"Goodso!" the professor said, delighted. "Is fine

shoot, not? And is all mine, Doktor Axeltree Breadno, mine mattematic kalkulätted!"

"But, Professor, blowing up London!"

"London—not. Sönmal Kungspalast."

"Only the King's palace," Dido guessed. He nodded. "Croopus, that's mighty pretty aiming, I must say. But, honestly, Professor, you mustn't blow up the poor old King, must he, Pen? What harm's he ever done to you?"

"No, indeed, it would be very wrong," Penitence agreed.

But they seemed unable to convey this idea to the professor. "Is cleverness, not?" he kept saying. "Will being magnifibang!" He was so pleased with his amazing feat of having made a gun that would shoot right across the Atlantic and hit St. James's Palace that he could not see any wrong in it.

"He's looking forward to the bang," Dido said exasperatedly.

"Is being donderboom!" he agreed with an eager nod. "And will pushing—lookso—" He made a gesture on the globe with his finger, from Nantucket around Long Island to New York Harbor. It took them some time to see what he meant.

"You mean," said Dido at last, "that the whatd'you-callem—the kickback from the shot—will push Nantucket right round to that place, New York City?"

"Is so!" he said in triumph. "Is byggdegrit, not?"

"It certainly is! Just wait till the mayor hears this! It ought to change his notions about not interfering. 'We keep ourselves to ourselves on Nantucket.'" Dido couldn't help bursting into a fit of laughter. Then she sobered up. Pen was looking absolutely aghast.

"Push Nantucket all that way? But the houses would fall down!"

"That wouldn't be the half of it, I daresay," Dido said. "Think of the waves! Look, Prof, when's all this due to happen? When? Bang?" She pointed to the clock and a calendar.

He flew into a complicated explanation; they could understand only about one word in eighteen. They gathered there was some final calculation to be made, and then he kept saying, "Expectness skepp coming."

"Oh, I know," Dido said at last. "He's waiting for the ship, the *Dark Diamond*. She's bringing the cannonball."

"So, is so!" He counted on his fingers. "Tvo, tree day."

"Three days? We've not got much time, then. Lucky Doc Mayhew's coming back. And then you sail away in the ship, do you?"

"Skepp awaits hjere." He demonstrated on the map that the *Dark Diamond*, having delivered the cannonball, would hurry round to the other side of Cape Cod to avoid any tidal waves caused by the sudden displacing of Nantucket, and when things had settled down would collect the professor and take him home.

"Lucky thing!" said Dido with envy.

"You wishing withcome? I fixing."

Pen gave Dido an anxious look but did not speak.

"Oh, goodness," Dido said. "Thanks, Professor, but I can't leave till Pen's fixed up. Anyway, I'd just as soon not sail along of Mr. Slighcarp." Or Auntie Trib, she thought. "Much obliged for the offer, though."

The professor now politely took his leave, indicating that he would return next day to collect his dried clothes. He offered handfuls of golden guineas to the girls, but they shook their heads.

"Not if they're your pay for blowing up poor old Kingy," Dido said. Professor Breadno beamed at her uncomprehendingly, kissed her hand again, murmuring, "Excellenzchildren," and trotted off down the hill.

"Well!" Left alone, the girls stared at one another in amazement.

"I *said* they was a peevy lot," Dido remarked at length. "But I never thought they was as peevy as that. Blowing up St. James's Palace!"

"And moving our island! Without so much as a by your leave!"

There came a tap at the door. Both girls jumped guiltily, but it was only Nate.

"Anyone in?" he said, putting his head round the door. "Say, girls! Guess the news! Guess who's turned up?"

"The *Sarah Casket?*"

Dido wondered if it could be the real Aunt Tribulation, but did not say so.

"No, it ain't that. It's the old pink 'un!"

"The pink whale?"

"Where is she?"

"Off Squam Head, as plain as plain. She's a-diving and a-playing and a-carrying on like a porpoise; everyone from Polpis has been there watching all afternoon. Doc Mayhew's given strict instructions no one's to hurt her. Is Cap'n Casket awake?"

"I'll see," said Pen, and ran upstairs.

"He ought to get a sight of her," Dido said, "as soon as he is well enough to go out. I dessay she'd do him all the good in the world."

They tiptoed upstairs after Penitence.

"Papa," she could be heard saying softly, "Papa, are you feeling better?"

"Is that thee, Daughter? Why, where am I?"

"In your own bed at home, Papa."

"Why, so I am. I have been having strange dreams." He sighed. To Pen's fright, two tears formed in his eyes and rolled slowly down his cheeks. "I dreamed that I had caught up with her at last," he said sadly, "and that she welcomed me."

"Who, Papa?"

"The pink whale. It was but a dream, though."

"No, Papa, it wasn't a dream! It was true! And she is waiting for you now, off Squam Head, waiting to see you, so you must hurry and get better," Pen told him joyfully. But his response was disappointing.

"I know thee does it for the best, Daughter, but thee must not tell falsehoods. There is no pink whale. It was but a dream. Else why should I be here, at Soul's Hill, and not aboard the *Sarah Casket*? I have been ill and dreaming."

"But, Papa, it was no dream. Other people have seen her too—Nate saw her!"

"It was a dream," he said obstinately. And to himself he added with a groan, "Alack, and was the first time a dream, too? The little pink whale calf washed up on Quidnet Beach? Has all my life's search been but a fool's quest for a phantom?"

"But, Papa, truly, she is out there now off Squam Head. Indeed, she is!"

Two more tears stood in Captain Casket's eyes, but he shook them away angrily, hunched his shoulders, and turned his face to the wall. To all Pen's protestations he would merely reply, "I do not believe thee. It was a dream."

Poor Pen came sadly out to the others.

"Never mind," Dido comforted her. "Maybe Doc Mayhew'll be able to convince him tomorrow. You make him some nice porridge or broth, summat strengthening, now. Nate'll help me with the butter."

While they were churning, Dido quickly told Nate about the abominable plan to blow up King James III in his palace, and the disastrous effect this would have on the island of Nantucket.

He whistled in dismay. "Heave Nantucket right back against the mainland just so's they can swap one king for another? Sounds like plumb foolishness to me. Did you tell the doc?"

"No," Dido said crossly. "He wouldn't listen to me. He thinks little girls tell fairy tales. You'll have to tell him tomorrow, Nate. Maybe he'll pay attention when he hears Nantucket's going to end up in New York Harbor."

"Guess so!"

"I hoped he'd know Aunt Tribulation was a faker," Dido went on, "but she turned him round her finger, smooth as pie, pretending to remember when he pushed her in the creek. He was fooled."

"Does Pen know she's really Miss Slighcarp?"

"No," Dido said. "I ain't told her. Young Pen's not much on play-acting; she'd give the whole game away."

"Oh, well, I'll be along in the morning early, before the doc gets here. 'Night!" Nate jumped onto his pony, which he had left tethered in the yard, and kicked it into a canter.

"Goodnight," Dido called. She turned back into the

dairy to get a pat of butter for supper—and stood still, petrified with horror. Aunt Tribulation was there, standing in the shadows behind the oil lamp. The upward-slanting light gave her face a most sinister expression.

"Oh!" Dido stammered. "I d-didn't know—that is, I th-thought you was asleep in the parlor."

"I *was* asleep," Aunt Tribulation said menacingly. "But I have woken up now, as you see. And I have overheard the most curious conversation!"

As Dido still gazed at her, frozen with indecision—how much had she heard, would there be time to shout after Nate and warn him?—Aunt Tribulation turned her head sharply and said, "Ebbo, deal with this one. And make no mistake about it—deal with her *for good!*"

A black bag came down over Dido's head, smothering her.

CHAPTER NINE

Kidnaped. Captain Casket is taken for a walk. Pen meets the doctor. The pink whale meets her friend. Breakfast on the beach.

DIDO STRUGGLED FURIOUSLY inside the sack, but somebody tied her hands in front of her, so she was helpless. When she tried to run, the long sack, which came down to her ankles, tripped her; she fell to the ground and lay there winded and gasping.

Low voices were speaking nearby. She heard Aunt Tribulation: "Did you get the boy, too, Brother?"

The answer was a grunt which could have been yes or no.

"That miserable little Breadno has been blabbing," Aunt Tribulation went on. "You can never trust scientists or foreigners, curse them! They've no sense. I always said it was a mistake to employ him."

"My dear, it was essential," Mr. Slighcarp's voice remonstrated. "He is the greatest European expert on guns. Without him we could never have made the necessary calculations."

"Greatest European expert he may be," Aunt Tribulation snapped, "but in all other ways the man's a

plain fool, whatever heathen country he comes from.
We should have kept a closer watch on him. Luckily,
it's only got as far as the children; they were to have
told Mayhew tomorrow. That has been stopped in
time. But Breadno is too big a risk; he'll have to be
dealt with too. Has he finished his final calculations?"

"He's just sighting the gun now, and calculating
the charge, back at the hut," Mr. Slighcarp's voice
said. "We'll make him work right through the night;
it shouldn't take him more than another three or
four hours. But, Sister, are you sure we shall be able
to fire the gun without him?"

"Of course we shall, ninnyhammer," she said impatiently. "Anybody can let off a gun, once it is aimed
and the amount of charge is calculated. He'll be no
loss. In any case, I was planning to leave him behind
on the island after the gun was fired; there'd have
been little sense in risking our necks returning to
pick him up. I'll fire it now, if you like; only mind
you pick *me* up."

"Very well." He sounded relieved at this sugges-
tion. "The rest of us will go on board *Dark Diamond*
as soon as the gun is loaded, and stand off round
Cape Cod in case of tidal waves. Then we'll come
back afterward to pick you up, wherever you've got
to. What shall we do with the prisoners, take them on
the ship too?"

"Has she been sighted yet?"

"No, I can't think what delays her," he said vex-
edly.

"Storms, perhaps. In any case," said the false Aunt
Tribulation, "there'd be no point in taking the
prisoners on board. We don't want to keep them; we
want to get rid of them. Tie a rock to their feet and

drop them over Sankaty Cliff when the tide is high."

Dido's hair stood on end when she heard this cold-blooded order. She struggled fiercely but in vain.

"Supposing the professor doesn't finish his sums till tomorrow morning? We can hardly toss them over the cliff in broad daylight. There might be people about watching for the whale."

"Shut them in the lighthouse till dark, then," she said impatiently. "The lighthouse keeper goes off at dawn, and you know where he keeps the key."

"Under a rock—yes, that would answer," he said, considering. "What about the third child—Casket's daughter—"

Dido held her breath.

"I heard the other girl say she knows nothing." Dido breathed again, remembering how she had told Nate in the dairy that Pen was unaware of Aunt Tribulation's real identity. Evidently, Aunt Tribulation had taken this to mean that Pen knew nothing about the plot at all. Lucky for Pen, Dido thought.

"She had better be left here," Aunt Tribulation went on. "Doctor Mayhew, when he returns, would think it strange if she were not in attendance on her father."

"On you, you mean," Mr. Slighcarp said sourly. "Oh, yes, it's very nice for you up here, waited on hand and foot by those children, while we pig it in the forest!"

"Don't be ridiculous, Brother. You know it was quite out of the question that I should camp with you in the forest; it would be most unsuitable." He made a sneering remark, but she ignored it and said, "I will think of some story to account for the absence of the other two, should anyone ask."

"Casket knows nothing about us?"

"Not he. His wits are clean gone."

"It must have been a shock for you when he turned up."

"In his present state, it was all for the best," she said calmly. "If my own *brother* accepts me, no one else can have any doubts."

"Suppose he recovers?"

"He is hardly likely to do so before we leave. He keeps jabbering blubber-headed stuff about pink whales."

"That's not so blubber-headed," Mr. Slighcarp said dryly. "She's there off Squam Head. There were crowds on the shore yesterday watching her. If she comes farther south we may have to change our plans; we can hardly unload the stuff from *Dark Diamond* with a whole lot of jobberknolls watching."

"In that case, you'd better choose some other point to dispose of the prisoners."

"It will be all right so long as it's dark," he said. "And we must be at Sankaty, anyway, to watch for the ship; we arranged to exchange signals there; then she'll heave to a mile off the coast, and we'll go out by boat as if we were after bass and collect the stuff."

"Very well. Send me a message as soon as she is sighted. You'd better get back to Breadno now and see that he is kept to work and doesn't wander off again looking for nighthawks or something else foolish. The sooner those prisoners are disposed of, the easier I shall feel; we don't want fuss and inquiries at this end spoiling our plans at the last minute."

Dido was now rudely dragged to her feet. The enveloping sack was hitched up so that she had the use of her legs and she was forced to walk by repeated prods

in the back. Her bound hands were buckled onto a
dangling strap. In a moment she realized that this
was the pony's stirrup. So they must have got Nate,
she thought dismally; he's probably on the other side
of the pony. She still could not see, because of the
sack over her head (it was a flour sack, and she kept
sneezing as the loose flour sifted down). Now we are
in the basket, she thought, how the mischief will
we get out of this fix? What'll Pen do when I don't
come back? Aunt Tribulation will tell her some tale,
so she won't worry for hours. Will she have the sense
to tell Doc Mayhew about the gun when he comes tomorrow? Yes, she'll probably have that much sense.
But will Doc Mayhew believe her? And suppose Aunt
Tribulation catches her at it? And even if he does believe her, that probably won't be in time to help Nate
and me and poor old Breadno. We'll be feeding the
fishes before they guess what's happened unless we
can work ourselves loose somehow. Oh, well, let's
hope old Breadno takes a devil of a long time over
those final calculations of his.

Immersed in these gloomy thoughts she trudged
along. The going was much rougher now; they had
left the track. Bushes and brambles caught her legs,
so she guessed they must be approaching the forest.
Presently they halted, and there was a long wait while
the pony stamped and shifted impatiently. Dido was
desperately tired and longed to sit down, but the
strap that attached her hands to the stirrup was too
short to allow this; all she could do was to lean
against the pony, grateful for its warmth in the chilly
night air. In the end she did fall into a sort of doze
on her feet, regardless of the awkward position. When
she next opened her eyes she was surprised to find

daylight filtering through the loose mesh of the flour sack. Presently footsteps approached and there were some faint protesting cries, which ceased abruptly; evidently poor Professor Breadno had been added to the roll of prisoners. Dido felt sorry for him and remorseful that she had been the cause of the gang's decision to dispose of him. But, she thought, he shouldn't have invented the gun. I suppose he don't see the harm in it; he's like a child.

Now the procession moved forward steadily for a considerable distance; Dido, stiff and aching all over, thought they might have gone three or four miles when at length they halted again and their captors conferred in low voices.

"Too late to chuck 'em now; broad daylight and somebody might come along. Besides, it ain't full tide yet; no water at foot of cliff."

Thank the Lord that Breadno took so long over his sums, Dido thought.

"Any sign of the ship yet?" a voice asked hoarsely.

"Yes, there's a sail to south'ards that looks like her."

"What the blazes is she doing down thataway? No wonder she's behind schedule," another voice complained.

"Gale blew her off course, maybe."

"Has the lighthouse keeper left yet?" This was Mr. Slighcarp.

"Yes, half an hour ago."

"Bring them along, then; best carry them the last bit. Lucky we put them in flour bags and the weather's a bit thick; if anyone happens along, we're just delivering flour to the lighthouse."

Mr. Slighcarp laughed sourly.

Dido was picked up and slung over somebody's shoulder, carried about a hundred yards in a very jolting and uncomfortable manner, and then thumped down roughly onto a stone floor. Something—another body—fell heavily on top of her. She wondered if it was Nate or Breadno. Then she heard footsteps retreating.

Have we been left alone? she wondered. Is there a guard? If so, he's keeping mighty quiet. I'll wait a little and see if he makes any sound; if not, I'll try to wriggle out of my sack.

She waited. There was total silence. She found it hard to keep her eyes from closing. I'll count to a hundred, she decided; then I'll move. Dunno when I've been so tired, though.

Counting was a mistake. The numbers slipped by more and more slowly . . . tied themselves in knots . . . began to run backward. Before she had reached forty, Dido was asleep.

The pony's footsteps had died away down the track. Aunt Tribulation turned and went back into the house. A delicious smell of broth filled the kitchen. She could hear the voice of Penitence upstairs in Captain Casket's room.

"Try to take a little more, Papa dear! To please me! Just a spoonful and a cracker. That's it—famous! Now you may lie down and sleep."

In a moment or two Pen appeared, looking very white and fatigued, with the empty bowl and plate.

"Well, miss!" Aunt Tribulation snapped. "I notice you make broth for your father but none for your poor old aunt, who's had charge of you all this time. Fine gratitude, I must say!"

"I'm sorry, Aunt," Penitence said tiredly. She pushed the hair off her forehead. "There is plenty more broth in the pot if you would like it. I can heat it up in a moment."

"Very well. Make haste!"

"Yes, Aunt." And Pen added gently, looking Aunt Tribulation straight in the face, "Poor Aunt, is your rheumatism very bad?"

"Mind your own business, miss!"

"Where's Dido?" Pen asked, as she put the broth pot on the stove.

"The cow got loose again. Nate offered to help her search, and they may not be back for a long time. You had best go to bed when you have washed up those dishes."

"I shall sit with Papa." Penitence poured broth into a bowl, adding a pinch of herbs and spices, and set it before Aunt Tribulation.

Then she quietly said goodnight and went up to the captain's room.

Aunt Tribulation sat at the kitchen table, grim and erect; slowly, because it was so hot, she sipped at the steaming broth.

Captain Casket suddenly woke up and looked about his room. The whale-oil lamp was still burning brightly, but daylight was beginning to creep past the curtains. He saw his daughter Penitence sitting at the foot of the bed. She was very pale.

"How do you feel now, Papa?" she asked in a low voice.

"I am better, Daughter, I thank thee, after that excellent broth and the good sleep it brought. I feel myself again."

"Do you *indeed*, Papa? Truly? Well enough to get up and take a walk?"

"Take a walk?" he repeated in bewilderment. "Why, what o'clock is it, then?"

"Not long after dawn."

"Strange time for a walk, Daughter?"

"No, Papa, it is very urgent—it is dreadfully important. Can you, do you think? Can you try?"

"What for, my child?"

"I will tell you when we are on our way. Please, Papa! I would not ask you if it were not so important. But if you cannot come I shall have to go on my own, and I do not like to leave you."

Captain Casket sat up and found himself fairly strong. "I shall do well enough, I thank thee, child," he said, when Pen offered to help him dress, so she retreated to the kitchen and packed a basket of food.

"Why, who is this?" Captain Casket said when he came downstairs.

"Hush!"

Penitence laid her finger on her lips and dragged him to the door. "I will tell you outside." He followed her, puzzled but complying.

When they were well away from the farm, Pen turned to the right and took the track leading towards Sankaty.

"Now!" she said. "I will explain everything, Papa. But first, did you really not know that lady sleeping in the kitchen?"

"Never saw her in my life before," declared Captain Casket.

"She is not my Aunt Tribulation?"

"That lady? No, indeed, nor in the least like her!

Tribulation is much shorter, with black hair and eyes."

"Is she? I had not remembered. But I suppose," Pen said thoughtfully, "I *was* only three the time I saw her. Well, Papa, that lady has been calling herself 'Aunt Tribulation' and living at the farm for the last month."

"I do not understand!" he said, passing a hand over his forehead. "Passing herself off as my sister Tribulation? But that is infamous behavior! Then, where is my sister?"

"I do not know, Papa."

"This is an outrage! We must go back at once and demand to know what she means by it, and where Tribulation is. Some harm may have come to her!"

"Wait, Papa, listen. I have not told you all yet. That is not nearly the worst. Yesterday Dido and I helped a man who had fallen into the cranberry bog. He is Professor Breadno, a foreign scientist, and he has made a gun in the Hidden Forest which is going to shoot a shot right across to London and kill the King of England."

Captain Casket sat down abruptly in a clump of broom. "I am *not* better," he said mournfully. "I am having wild delusions. I think my own daughter is telling me about a gun which will fire across the Atlantic. Next I shall be seeing pink whales."

Pen pulled him to his feet.

"Yes, you will, Papa, but please listen, this is true! It is a wicked plot by the English Hanoverians to get rid of King James."

"But why," asked her father doggedly. "Not that I believe a word of this, mind thee, but why do they come all the way to Nantucket to fire at King James? Why not just do it across the Thames?"

"Why?" Pen said impatiently. "Because nobody over here will bother to stop them. But in London I suppose the King's soldiers would grab them if they so much as showed their faces. But that is not the worst, Papa."

"Speak on then, Daughter."

"Last night," said Pen breathlessly, "I went out to the dairy for some butter, and what do you think I saw? The woman who calls herself 'Aunt Tribulation' was there, and she and Mr. Slighcarp put a sack over poor Dido's head and tied her hands up with rope, and I heard Aunt Tribulation say that Dido and Nate were to be thrown over Sankaty Cliff."

"Why should they want to do that?" asked Captain Casket in perplexity.

"Because Dido and Nate had found out about their gun and were going to get Doctor Mayhew to stop them. And that woman who pretends to be Aunt Tribulation is really Mr. Slighcarp's sister. I heard her call him 'brother.'"

"Slighcarp? Is he, too, involved in this? I always thought him a sly, foxy-faced fellow. I was glad enough when he failed to turn up for this trip."

"Mr. Slighcarp was helping get the gun ready in the Hidden Forest. Oh, Papa, I was so frightened when I heard the things they said! I nearly screamed out to them to let poor Dido and Nate go, but I knew they would only put *my* head in a bag too, and then there would be nobody to help them, or to look after you, Papa."

"So what did thee do then, Daughter?"

"I crept away in the shadows with my butter dish—

it is fortunate that I am not very big. And, then, luckily, Aunt Tribulation—I mean Miss Slighcarp—asked
me for some of your broth. So I dosed it with some of
the poppy juice that Doctor Mayhew had left for you,
and she went off to sleep in the kitchen, as you saw."
Here Penitence could not help giggling at the
thought of having successfully put Aunt Tribulation
to sleep twice in twenty-four hours.

"Dear me, Daughter. Was that judicious?"

"But, Papa, what else could I do? They are going
to throw Dido and Nate and Professor Breadno off
Sankaty Cliff unless we do something to stop them. So
as soon as Aunt Trib—Mr. Slighcarp's sister—was
asleep and you were peaceful, Papa, I crept out of
the house and went to the forest and warned the professor to take as long over his calculations as he pos-
sibly could. I do not think he precisely understood
why I wished him to do so, but when I explained that
the lives of my friends depended on it, and gave him
some molasses candy, he agreed."

"Thee went to the camp of these villains in the
forest? But, Daughter, was thee not afraid?"

"Yes, I was," Penitence said in a low tone. "I was
dreadfully afraid."

"And did the others not stop thee speaking to this
man?"

"No, because they had left him alone in a little hut
and were sitting outside round a fire. So I stole in
very quietly, and he was very surprised to see me."

"Alack!" said Captain Casket. He had halted, leaning heavily on his daughter's shoulder. "Child, I am
not so well as I thought. I must sit and rest awhile.
Perhaps thee had best go on to Sankaty without me.
Yet, what can one frail child do against such evil? I

shall be in dread for thee." His legs failed him and he sank into a clump of bayberry.

"Oh, Papa!" cried Penitence in distress. "Can you really go no farther? Look, it is not much more than a mile now to Sankaty. You can see the white tower."

"Child, I have outplayed my strength. The fever was a short one but sharp while it lasted."

"Oh, what shall I do?" Penitence wrung her hands. "I shall have to go on, Papa. I must try to help Dido and Nate. They have been so good to me."

"Yes, thee must. I shall pray for thy safe return. Ask help of anyone thee may encounter—yet, it is not likely that many will be abroad at this hour," he said doubtfully.

"There may be some," said Pen with more optimism, "because of the pi—" She checked herself, gave her father a tender kiss, and hurried on towards the foot of the slope at the top of which Sankaty Lighthouse stood on the cliff edge like a pointing finger.

By great good luck, Penitence had not gone far when she heard the thud of hoofs. Crossing her path ahead lay the road from Polpis to Sankaty; to her left she saw a cart proceeding at a smart pace. By running her fastest and waving a handkerchief she was able to attract the attention of the driver, who slowed to a halt as she reached the road.

"Well, bless my soul if it isn't little Penitence Casket!" cried a cheerful voice. "What are you doing out so early? Like all the rest of Nantucket, come for a sight of the pink whale? She's a bit farther up the coast, child, towards Squam, but heading this way. How's my patient this morning?"

It was Doctor Mayhew, driving Mungo.

"Oh, Doctor Mayhew!" cried Pen thankfully. "I was never so glad to see anybody in all my life, never! Will you help me, please?"

"Of course I will, child. I was just on my way to visit your father, soon as I've seen a patient in 'Sconset. I spent the night with Mrs. Pardon at Polpis, and then, thought I, I'll just have another look at this famous pink whale and, if she's still there and old Jabez Casket is able, I'll take him to see her; a sight like that might be just the thing to put him on his legs again."

"Oh, yes!" cried Pen. "It was what I thought, too! But when I told Papa that she had been seen he would not believe me. He thought he had been dreaming."

"He'll believe the evidence of his own eyes, I suppose. And ears. Listen!"

He checked Pen, who was dying to be off, and they both stood silent. Above the hushing of the sea beyond the cliff could be heard a strange noise—a most mournful bellow, rising sometimes to a whistle, then sinking again to a kind of discontented mutter.

"What is it?" Pen asked, momentarily distracted from her anxiety.

"Why, it's the old pink 'un, grizzling away out there in the ocean. It's my belief," continued the doctor, "that she misses your pa and is a-calling for him. And the sooner he sees her the better, in my opinion."

"Will you help me fetch him?" Pen said eagerly. "He is not far from here. We started to walk to Sankaty, but Papa's strength failed him."

"Walk to Sankaty? Child, are you out of your wits? What possessed you to do such a thing?"

"Oh, sir, there are wicked men on Nantucket who are going to throw Dido and Nate into the sea off Sankaty Cliff. They have shut them up in the lighthouse till this evening. Will you help me let them out?"

"Eh, bless my soul," the doctor said in astonishment. "What imaginations you young 'uns do have. Only yesterday that friend of yours was telling me all about some gun in the forest. Says I, 'that's no gun, child, but the biggest telescope between here and California.' "

"But it *is* a gun! They are in the lighthouse! If you come with me you will see!"

"Dear, dear," said the doctor. "Ah, well, I always say it does no harm to humor people in their fancies. What shall we do first, then, pick your father up or go to the lighthouse?"

"Oh, the lighthouse, please!" Pen said, clutching his arm in her anxiety. "Every moment may be important."

"Very well, we'll see how fast this canny old mule of yours can go if he's pushed."

Mungo was cooperative, and it took them only another ten minutes to gallop up the hill to the lighthouse. The place seemed totally deserted. A chill wind blew the grasses and straggling shrubs which covered the sandhills roundabout; beyond the low cliff the ocean growled and whispered. The desolate bellow of the pink whale could still be heard farther north.

"Oh, quick!" whispered Pen, as the doctor tied Mungo to a railing. "Suppose we are too late!"

"What about the key, child?"

"I heard Mr. Slighcarp say that it was kept under a rock."

"It'll be close by the door, I reckon," grunted the doctor, and soon found it. "Well, now, where's these poor castaway captives of yours?" He thrust the big key into the lock, turned it, and pushed open the heavy door. "Anybody about?" he called, and walked in, with Pen close at his heels.

The round room was empty.

"You see," Doctor Mayhew said indulgently. "All imagination, as I was say—"

But Pen had darted in horror to a pile of flour sacks and bits of rope.

"*Look!*" White as a sheet she held up a length of rope. "There's blood on this! Doctor Mayhew! Do you think they've thrown them over already?"

"Thrown—hey! Let's have a look at that rope. Yes, that's blood, sure enough," he muttered, inspecting it. "And recent, too. It's hardly dry. What in tarnation's name has been going on around here? Can there be some truth in the child's story?" He stared at her in doubt.

"Hush!" whispered Pen with terrified eyes. "What's that sound?"

They listened, and both heard it: a step on the winding stair overhead.

Then all of a sudden a voice burst into song:

*"As I was a-walking down Wauwinet way
I met a young maiden and this she did say:
Oh, Pocomo's pretty and Quidnet is quaint,
But swimming on Surfside is fit for a saint!*

*And Madaket's modish and 'Sconset's sedate
And Shimmo is sheltered and Great Point is great—"*

"*Nate!*" cried Pen. "Nate, is that you?"

"It's never Penitence?" He came clattering down the stair and into sight. "And Doc Mayhew too! Well, of all the luck! Chop me into chowder, however did you get here?"

"Where's the others? Where's Dido? And Professor Breadno?"

"Just a-coming down," he said, grinning. "It's a powerful long stair. We'd been up top, trying to work out whether, if we tied all the bits of rope together, they'd be long enough to let one of us down to unlock the door from the outside. Dido thought yes. Professor Breadno thought not. I'm glad we didn't have to try. Hey!" he yelled up the stair. "Pen's here with the doc. Come on down!"

"*Penny!*"

Dido shot down the last round of the spiral stair like a whirlwind, threw herself at Pen, and hugged her. "How did you do it? How did you know we was here? You *clever* little girl, Pen!"

Doctor Mayhew was staring at Nate's wrists. "So that's where the blood came from! Hey, boy, who's been gnawing at you?"

"Well, you see, sir, we was tied up. Dido and I managed to shuffle the sacks off each other—that took a plaguy long time, I can tell you—but we couldn't get our ropes undone, not nohow. So I rubbed through mine on the edge of the bottom stair, but it left my wrists kind of chawed-up."

"And then he undid me and the professor," Dido explained.

"I'll put something on those wrists for you right away, my boy. But where are the miscreants now?"

"They sighted their schooner, the *Dark Diamond*. I heard them talking outside. They were planning to go out to her in a dory, as if they was after fish. Guess that's the dory you can see about a mile to south'ard now. You can get a famous view of the old pink 'un from the top of the tower; she's running down this way like a Saratoga winner—hear her bellow?"

"Ja—hwalnn!" exclaimed Professor Breadno enthusiastically. "Ismistibiggn hwalln!" He had been more than a little subdued since his recent experience, but the sight of Rosie appeared to have cheered him up.

"Oh, this is Professor Breadno," Nate told the doctor. "He was going to let off the gun for the Hanoverians, but he told Dido and Pen about it, so his friends fixed to chuck him over the cliff in case he told anyone else. Nice lot, ain't they?"

"So there really is a gun, my boy? It is not a telescope, not a fairy tale of the young ladies?"

"Oh, no, it's there right enough, sir. And the professor says it's capable of firing across to London."

"Königsbang, monstershoot," the professor put in proudly.

"So we've got to stop them, haven't we?" Dido said.

"Well, but that ain't so easy, my dear," Doctor Mayhew objected. "For one thing, it's none of our affair if the English choose to blow each other up. For another, there's precious few able-bodied men on the island—every manjack of them is off whaling, and we've nothing but young children and old crocks like myself, and whale widows."

"But Doctor!" exclaimed Pen. "You haven't heard the worst yet! When those wicked men let off the gun it will blow Nantucket right back against the mainland—right into New York City Harbor!"

Doctor Mayhew slowly turned purple. It was a fearsome sight.

"What did you say?" he bellowed. "Just repeat that, will you?"

"It's true, Doc!"

There were maps and charts on the wall. Professor Breadno was pleased to demonstrate how, when the shot was fired across Nova Scotia, the backthrust would send the island of Nantucket sliding southwestward around Long Island to bump into New York City Harbor.

"She ain't so tight on her moorings, I guess," Nate said. "Being mostly sand."

"Great guns! Why didn't you tell me that before? *Push our island over into that crowd of money-grabbing roustabouts and frauds in New York?* Why, we'd have a lawsuit from here to doomsday before we ever got it out of their clutches again. What would all the whaling captains say to me when they came back from their voyages and found Nantucket had moved? This puts a different complexion on the whole matter!"

"What'll we do, then?"

"We'll have to go into it very thoroughly," Doctor Mayhew said, taking deep breaths to calm himself down.

Here Penitence said in a small voice, "Please, what about Papa?"

The doctor started.

"Quite right, my dear, quite right. In the emotion of the moment I had forgotten about him. We must go to his aid at once. Nate, just run up and make sure those scoundrels are well away, so that we can leave the lighthouse in safety."

Nate soon reported that both the *Dark Diamond*
and the dory had shifted south; the *Dark Diamond*
was almost out of sight round the corner of the island
at Tom Never's Head, and the dory was pursuing
her.

"Guess they don't want to get mixed up with the
old pink 'un," he said. "She's middling close now;
hear her whistle?"

Indeed, the whale was now letting off regular
blasts, like the siren of a lightship, almost as if she
were trying to attract somebody's attention. With one
accord the whole party moved outside to look for her.

"Why, there's Papa!" cried Pen joyfully. "He must
have felt himself sufficiently rested to follow me.
Papa, Papa! Do you feel all right now? Are you sure
that you have not overtired yourself?"

"No, Daughter, no," Captain Casket said absently.
He moved towards the group.

The hillside where they stood sloped up quite
steeply past the lighthouse to the cliff edge, so that it
was not possible to get a view of the sea until one
stood on the very summit.

"What is that sound?" said Captain Casket.

"Take care, Papa!" cried Pen anxiously. She darted
to him and held his arm, supporting him tenderly.
They moved on together and stood at the top of the
cliff.

A great sigh burst from Captain Casket.

"Oh!" he said brokenly. "I am dreaming again. I
must be! But it is a beautiful dream!"

"No, Papa, it is no dream! We all see her too."

"And ain't she half carrying on," said Dido. "Gosh-
swoggle, ain't she got no *dignity*? You'd think a grown
whale would be ashamed to act so."

The pink whale was indeed giving an exuberant display of rapture at meeting her old friend Captain Casket. It was a beautiful and touching sight. She leapt clean out of the water a great many times, as if bent on demonstrating how high she could go; she repeatedly dived and came up, she rolled playfully from side to side waving her flukes and, as Dido said, "ogling the captain like an orange-girl."

"I am not dreaming?" Captain Casket said.

"No, old friend, no, she's there, sure enough," Doctor Mayhew assured him. "Looks like she remembers you, all right, too!"

"Then it is—it *is* the little whale calf that I put back into the sea all those long years ago! And I have not been dreaming—then or now. I always wondered if I should see her again—hoped I should—and then, one year at Fiji when I heard the islanders speak of a great pink sea dragon—I wondered if it could be she! I have been seeking her ever since. Oh," said the captain brokenly, "I must go down to her!"

"Pray be very careful, Papa!"

"Why don't we all go down?" Doctor Mayhew suggested. "Didn't I see you with a basket of food, Pen? How about breakfast on the beach? I need a bite o' food to soothe me—help me to marshal my thoughts. Those ruffians are not likely to come back while *she's* out there. And it's not a sight to miss."

So Pen fetched the food from the cart while Dido and Nate prospected for a path down the cliff, and then the whole party descended to the beach. Captain Casket made straight for the edge of the ocean, and Pen had much ado to prevent his wading in, so eager was he to approach as close as possible to the pink whale—who, luckily, saw his intention and swam in near to the land; and so these two friends gazed at one another with the utmost delight and mutual satisfaction.

"Could you give her a hint not to come too close, sir?" Nate said anxiously. "It'd be the devil to pay dragging her off if she got beached; I daresay she'll weigh all of a hundred and fifty tons."

"She is a fine figure of a whale," murmured Captain Casket blissfully. But he roused himself to make some warning gestures, and the pink whale evidently understood these, for she swam to and fro parallel with the shore, letting out a series of loving bellows, without coming too near.

"Well, it's most uncommon, I'm bound to say," Dido remarked. "But if I don't get summat to eat soon you might just as well bury me on this beach, for I shan't be able to climb up the cliff again. What've you got in your basket, Penny?"

Pen had large numbers of hard-boiled eggs and buttered biscuits, molasses tarts, and for the captain a stone jug of broth, which Dido and Nate heated up over a driftwood fire. The broth was all he would take; after that he stood at the edge of the surf throwing hard-boiled eggs to Rosie, who caught them with the grace of a porpoise. Doctor Mayhew opened his black bag and brought out a large leather bottle of ginger-jub, which he passed round for the party's refreshment.

"Never go on my rounds without it," he said. "If medicine won't help a man, this will. Many's the fellow digging clams today who'd ha' been buried long ago but for a dram of ginger-jub." It was, indeed, powerful stuff.

While they were eating, Dido said, "Now, Penny, I wants to hear all about how you came to be traipsing over the moors at sunup with your pa, a-rarin' to rescue us, instead of snoring in your bed like a good girl. How the mischief did you know where we was?"

Pen explained how she had overheard the scene in the dairy.

"And you mean to say you bamboozled old Misery so she never guessed you knew? Why, Pen, I never thought you had it in you," exclaimed Dido handsomely. "You're a walking wonder, girl! And slipped another dose of holusbolus in her skilly? She'll surely think she's got sleeping sickness! Oh, dear, I haven't laughed so much since Mr. Slighcarp fell over the cutting spade!"

"Order!" said Doctor Mayhew severely. "Now, has everybody finished eating? Nate! Stop throwing eggs to the whale. This is a serious occasion. We have got to think how to prevent those rapscallions from heaving our island into the middle of New York Harbor!"

CHAPTER TEN

*Ways and means. Penitence eavesdrops. Aunt Trib-
ulation is suspicious. The rocket. The gun's last ride.*

"Now," SAID Doctor Mayhew, absently tipping the
last of the ginger-jug down his gullet, "how are we
going to stop them firing this gun?"

"Is not firing kungscannon?" exclaimed Professor
Breadno woefully. "Is not having bigbang?"

"Your big bang, my dear Professor, would leave
this island in a devilish undesirable location."

"Could firing otherwards round world mayhaps?"
the professor said hopefully. "I fixing nordwestbang."

"No, no, Professor, that would push us out into the
middle of the Atlantic, right over to Spain probably.
Can't you see, we don't want the gun fired at *all.*"

The professor's face fell.

"Besides," Dido pointed out kindly, "you really
can't shoot poor old King James, you know!"

"Na, na, na, snat Kung Jimsbangen, 'sKung George-
bangen. King George the Fourth!"

"King George the Fourth?" said Dido, bewildered.
"But we haven't *got* a King George! It's King James
the Third, bless his wig!"

The professor shook his head and burst into a flood of refutal, mostly in his own incomprehensible language, which it took some time to disentangle.

"I see what it is," Dido said at length. "Those peevy culls have been leading him up the garden path, making him believe there was a Hanoverian king on the throne because he's really *against* the Hanoverians and they wanted him to make the gun for them. Talk about pitching the double! What a lot of swindlers! Can you explain to him, Doc?"

It took some time to get across to the professor that there was already the sort of king he preferred on the English throne and therefore no need to shoot anyone off it; in the end he was convinced but greatly disappointed.

"Firing at sönn, at mönn, at stare?" he suggested as a last, forlorn hope.

"No, Breadno, that just *wouldn't do*. It would sink us. We'd go right under water. Have a bit of sense, can't you?" remonstrated the doctor.

Poor Professor Breadno sighed heavily and stumped away from the council down to the edge of the waves, where he stood skipping stones and gazing mournfully at Rosie, who, exhausted by her great aquabatic display, was resting comfortably in the swell, her tiny eyes fixed on Captain Casket with a look of great devotion.

"You say the gun is now all ready to fire, and the professor's presence is not needed?" Doctor Mayhew said to Dido.

"That's right. Aunt Trib—Miss Slighcarp said she would fire it. They only need the cannonball, and that's being delivered today. Then they plan to go back on board the ship, tipping us over the cliff on the way, I dessay, and skedaddle till the rumpus has died down, before coming back to pick up the gunner. They wasn't aiming to pick up poor old Breadno at all; I wonder if they'll leave Auntie Trib behind too?"

"So," said Doctor Mayhew thoughtfully, "as we haven't enough able-bodied men on the island to deal with a whole shipload of desperate ruffians, our best plan would be somehow to get rid of the gun itself before they can fire it."

"But, Doc, it's *huge!*" said Dido. "It's about a mile long, and as thick as a tree! I don't see how you'll ever get it moved if you've got no help but grannies and young 'uns and whaling widders."

"No more do I at present," Doctor Mayhew said frankly. "But somehow it must be done, so we had all better set our wits to work."

For a long time nobody spoke. They sat frowning in the silence of intense thought.

"We couldn't stuff the barrel full o' summat?" Dido suggested doubtfully.

"That might lead to a most disastrous explosion," Doctor Mayhew said.

"Cut the gun into sections—no, that would take too long," Nate muttered.

Several hours slipped by in fruitless discussion. Nate paced about the beach in circles, staring at the ground.

At last Pen said, "Sheep."

"*Sheep,* Penny?"

"There are such a lot on the island. Could they not be put to some use? Harnessed to the gun and made to drag it away?"

"Dunnamany ropes you'd need," Dido said kindly. "Have another try."

Nate, who had wandered near, strolled down to the edge of the waves and skipped stones with the professor.

"Or we could bury—no, that would not do," Pen sighed in discouragement.

"Hallo, what's bitten Nate and the professor?" Dido suddenly said.

Nate, apparently galvanized by an idea, had grabbed the professor's arm and was talking to him earnestly, using a lot of gestures, sometimes pointing out to sea. They buttonholed Captain Casket and brought him into the discussion. He nodded, at first doubtfully, then with confidence and animation.

"What's the lay?" called Dido. Nate came pounding back over the pebbles, with the others close behind him.

"We've got it! The very thing! We'll use the pink 'un."

"Old Rosie?" said Dido. "Why, o' course! She's just the article. Why, in Pharaoh's name, didn't we think of her sooner?"

"But how? How do you mean?" said Pen.

"Why, it was your notion of the sheep that put it into my head," Nate told her. "Tie a rope to her flukes, don't you see, and get her to haul the gun into the sea. It'd be as easy as a greased slide."

"But would it be *kind*?" said Penitence dubiously.

"Cap'n Casket's agreeable to the idea. Says he don't think it'd upset her too much."

"We'd need an uncommonly strong rope, and a long one," Doctor Mayhew observed.

"There's the lifeguard rope," Nate said. "That's

best new five-inch Manila, and there's nigh on two mile of it."

"We'll need all of that. Now let's think of how we'd go about this. One party would have to make an end of the rope fast to the gun, while Captain Casket and somebody else must row out to the whale with the other end. We can use the lifeguard's dory. I had best be with the captain, who must obviously remain here on the shore so that the whale does not swim away before we are ready. Nate, you had better go with Professor Breadno and tie the rope to the gun; the professor will know the most suitable place to make fast."

Nate saw a difficulty.

"How're we going to shift the rope? That coil's powerful heavy."

"In Mungo's cart," Dido suggested. "We can all lift it in, and then it will unroll as you go."

"We can't take the cart all the way to the forest; if there's anybody left on guard they'd spot us."

"No, but you'll have unrolled a lot of rope by the time you get there; it won't be so heavy. You can leave the cart about half a mile away and roll the coil along the last bit. There are sheepskins in the cart; put those on your shoulders and meander through the scrub a bit aimlesslike and stooping; anybody watching from the forest'll think you're a sheep. I'll come with you to keep a lookout," Dido volunteered.

"We really ought to try to find out when they aim to fire," Doctor Mayhew said. "If Miss Slighcarp's going to do it, we only have to keep an eye on her movements, and as soon as she starts for the forest we'll know. Who could do that?"

All eyes turned on poor Penitence, who became

rather pale, swallowed once or twice, and then said valiantly, "I'll do it. I don't mind. That is, if, Doctor Mayhew, you'll promise to look after Papa."

"Penny you're a real bang-up hero," Dido said warmly. "I wish I could come with you, but if Auntie Trib was to see I'd got out of the lighthouse she'd twig the whole lay in a minute. But you can pretend you know nothing about anything and just act like a saphead—try to delay her from going to the forest if she seems liable to start too soon, before Nate and the cap'n are ready and we've got the gun away. Can you keep her till a couple of hours after dark?"

"How should I delay her?" asked Pen nervously.

"Why, talk to her, distract her, ask her advice about summat—ask her how to make wedding cake or some blame thing."

"And supposing she wants to know where I've been and where Papa is, what shall I tell her?"

"Why, you can tell the truth. Say Doc Mayhew reckoned as how it would do your pa good to have a look at the pink whale and that he's a-sitting on Sankaty Beach. That sounds innocent and harmless and will put her off the scent. Say he's a-goin' to spend the night with Doc Mayhew."

"Very well," said Pen, wan but resolute.

Everything was now in train. The whole party helped to lift the lifeguard rope, which was kept coiled in a chest at the foot of the lighthouse, onto Mungo's cart. Then Doctor Mayhew and Captain Casket returned to the beach, dragging with them one end of the rope, while Nate, Dido, and Professor Breadno drove slowly away down the Polpis road, unrolling the coil as they went. They took Pen with them for a mile or so, and then she left them and struck off across the moors towards Soul's Hill.

"Poor Penny," said Dido, who waved vigorously as long as Pen was in sight. "I reckoned as how I'd teach her to stand up to Aunt Tribulation, but I never figured things would be quite as rugged as this. But she's coming up smiling, I will say; I'd never 'a thought Pen had so much gumption in her. Reckon her pa ought to be mighty well satisfied with her now, considering what a little puny moping thing she was on board ship. If he could take his mind off that blame whale o' hisn for five minutes, that is!"

The whale was still just visible, rocking like a pink blancmange in the breakers, and Nate began singing softly:

"Sweet whale of Nantucket, so rosy and nice,
As round and as pink as a strawberry ice—"

"That ain't stately enough," Dido said. "That don't give a proper notion of her at all."

"All right." Nate considered a moment or two, while a few more fathoms of rope unrolled.

"How about this, then?"

"Sweet whale of Nantucket, so pink and so round,
The pride of our island, the pearl of the Sound,
By Providence blest to our shores you were led,
Long, long may you gambol off Sankaty Head!"

"That's better," said Dido. "Though it was really Cap'n Casket she was led by, not Providence. I guess, really, all the time he thought he was following her, *she* was following *him*."

As Pen disappeared over a hill Dido said, with a sudden pang of anxiety, "Croopus, I do hope nothing don't go wrong when Penny gets to the farm. I wonder did we do right to send her?"

"Oh, I guess she'll be all right," Nate said.

Dusk had begun to fall when Penitence reached the farm. Nobody was in sight. The cows had been milked and turned out to pasture, probably by Mrs. Pardon. Penitence slipped quietly into the kitchen and then paused, as she heard voices coming from the parlor. The door was not quite closed.

". . . should be loaded by now," Mr. Slighcarp's voice said. "Thanks to that cursed whale and all the brats and old grannies swarming on the beach at Quidnet, we were obliged to slip right round to the south side of the island, which meant the men had to carry the shot a great deal farther from the landing place. We didn't want to risk anyone getting a sight of it."

"No, you were very right," his sister agreed. "Where is the *Dark Diamond* now?"

"Making north again, back to Quidnet. Just coasting along she's innocent enough—might be going back for another sight of the pink whale. We've another boat beached at Quidnet ready to take us all off to her when the gun's loaded."

"What delayed the ship so long?"

"They were chased all the way from the mouth of the Thames by a perditioned naval sloop, the *Thrush,* which several times nearly caught them; in order to give it the slip they were forced to beat right down to Trinidad."

"What happened to the sloop, then?" asked Miss Slighcarp uneasily.

"They lost her in the end; probably gave up and went back to report failure."

"It's as well we are now ready to fire."

"They could never have touched us on Nantucket; it's American soil. But we had best get away prudently and as fast as possible in case the sloop is still hanging about."

"What time shall I fire the gun?"

Penitence drew nearer to the door and listened intently.

Mr. Slighcarp did some calculating. "Hmm, there's a fair southwesterly, say fifteen knots, plus the trip to Quidnet. . . . Give us time to get away. Say, six hours. Better make it eight hours. Don't fire before midnight."

"Very well. I will fire at midnight exactly. Darkness suits me better," she said. "There is no risk of being seen on my way there. I don't want to be suspected before you come back to pick me up. As Tribulation Casket I am safe enough."

"Come to think," he said, "where is old Casket and the child?"

"Lord knows. The wretched, foggy sea air in this place makes me sleep like the dead; when I woke this morning it was late and they'd gone off somewhere. Mrs. Pardon, who came to milk, told me Doctor Mayhew proposed taking Casket to see the whale. I suppose that's where they are."

"Safe enough. Wasn't Mrs. Pardon worried about her boy?"

. "I said he and the other child had gone fishing. You'll deal with them?"

"We couldn't just leave them, I suppose?" he said.

"Fool! Use your wits! As soon as they speak to any-body, our whole plan comes crashing down. If the lighthouse keeper sees them—no, they must be dealt with."

"I'll see to it, then. On the way to the boat. I must hurry. One last thing—"

"Yes?"

The voices were approaching the door and Pen looked desperately round for a hiding place. There was just time to scramble into the clock.

"Should any emergency arise, so that it becomes necessary to fire *before* the time agreed, we will com-municate by these rockets. If we let off our rocket, fire the gun as soon as possible afterward. Likewise, if for some reason you need to fire earlier, send off your rocket first to warn us and we'll make for what shelter we can, wherever we are. But fire at all costs; we shall never have a better chance. The usurping Stuart monarch is bound to be in his palace tonight because tomorrow is the state opening of Parliament."

"I shall not fail."

She laid the rocket on the kitchen table, and two of them went out of the house. The sound of their voices was cut off by the door slamming.

Pen acted on a lightning impulse. She sprang out of the clock, seized the rocket, which was about the size of a French loaf, and dipped it, first one end, then the other, in a large jug of buttermilk. A bundle of lucifer matches lay with the rocket. She served them in the same manner. There was just time to climb back into the clock before Aunt Tribulation re-entered the house.

Pen was now in terror lest Aunt Tribulation ob-

serve the damp state of the rocket or should take it
into her head to wind the clock. Fortunately, she did
neither of these things but went upstairs. Seizing the
chance, Pen slipped out into the barnyard, first
cautiously reconnoitering to make sure that Mr.
Slighcarp had gone. He was visible in the distance,
walking down the track to Sankaty at a great pace.
Pen walked back into the kitchen, making as much
noise as possible, took a deep breath, and called up
the stairs, "Aunt? Aunt Tribulation? Are you there?"

"Penitence? Is that you?"

Aunt Tribulation—somehow Pen could not think
of her as Miss Slighcarp—came downstairs, looking
grim. To Pen's alarm, she had exchanged her usual
gingham for a black silk dress and a black, fringed
shawl. She carried an awe-inspiring bonnet ornament-
ed with small jet tombstones. She wore bottle-green
boots.

"Well!" she said. "What have you to say for yourself, miss? Where have you been all day? And where
is your father?"

"With Doctor Mayhew, ma'am, watching the pink
whale. You were asleep when we left—we did not like
to disturb you. Doctor Mayhew is keeping Papa at his
house tonight, but they—they thought I should come
home. Is Dido not back yet?"

"You can see she is not," Aunt Tribulation remarked severely. "Well, child, don't stand gaping—
there are plenty of tasks to be done. What's the
matter?"

"You are so fine, Aunt!"

"I shall be going out by and by," Aunt Tribulation
said carelessly. "Hurry now—feed the animals and
make some supper."

"Yes, ma'am."

As Pen fed the pigs and hens she was filled with anxious calculations. If Aunt Tribulation did not go off to fire the gun till midnight, that was excellent, for it should give Nate and the professor ample time to secure the rope, and for the pink whale to do her part. But what would happen when Mr. Slighcarp returned to Sankaty Lighthouse and found the captives had escaped? Almost certainly he would let off his rocket and Aunt Tribulation, alerted, would start out to fire the gun much earlier. Could she somehow be prevented from hearing or seeing the rocket? Pen hurried back to the house, leaving half the pigs screaming with rage because they had not been fed.

Aunt Tribulation was seated in the kitchen rocker, grimly swaying back and forth while she stared straight ahead; from the expression on her face she might have been enjoying the spectacle of St. James's Palace blowing sky-high. Pen began clanking pots and pans, putting bacon to hiss and splutter in a skillet, pounding sugar to break up the lumps.

"Don't make such a noise, child," Aunt Tribulation said. "I can't hear myself think. No, don't draw the curtains yet. It is too stuffy, and not quite dark. Leave them."

Reluctantly, Pen obeyed. She served Aunt Tribulation a large bowl of chowder and, taking some herself, began to eat it noisily.

"Don't gulp so, miss! You sound like a pig. And, talking about pigs, why are they squealing? I don't believe you can have fed them properly. Go and give them more to eat."

While Pen was outside there was a short, sharp report from the direction of Quidnet. A twisting snake of green light shot into the twilit sky and fell, scatter-ing sparks. Oh, my goodness! thought Pen. She hur-ried indoors.

Aunt Tribulation was hastily putting on her bon-net.

"Oh, please, Aunt, where are you going?"

"It's none of your business, miss. Mind you, wash the dishes now."

"Oh, but please—before you go—I want to ask you how to make wedding cake—"

"Have you gone *mad,* child? Pass my umbrella—there, by the flour crock."

"I mean," said poor Pen, "not wedding cake, I mean, please, would you give me some advice about my sampler? I should so like to do the sails in satin stitch, but I do not know how. Would you be so kind as to show me, and then I can sew it after I have fin-ished the dishes?"

Aunt Tribulation looked at her narrowly. "What's all this about? Wedding cake—samplers—*are you concealing something from me, Penitence?*"

"N-n-no, Aunt!"

Aunt Tribulation took a menacing step towards Pen, who winced back. But just at that moment the clock struck the half-hour. Aunt Tribulation ap-peared to recollect that time was too short for ques-tions.

"Make haste, then," she said. "Fetch the sampler."

Relieved, Pen ran up to her room, unaware that Aunt Tribulation followed behind with swift, silent steps. As Pen knelt to take the canvas from its tissue in her bottom drawer, she heard the key turn in her door. She had been locked in.

Darting to the window, she saw Aunt Tribulation

walk into the yard, putting the bundle of matches in her reticule, and set off with rapid strides towards the forest.

"Be-e-e-eh!" bleated Dido in Nate's ear. "Hallo! All rug?"

"Nearly done!" he whispered. "We made fast; the prof's just taking a last look. I think he can't hardly bear to say goodby to his gun. It was lucky we'd covered the rope with leaves and bits o' brish as we went—we'd hardly finished when two of those scoundrels come sloping past going towards Sankaty—on their way to drop our poor bodies over the cliff, I reckon. Wonder what they'll do when they find we're gone?"

"Get lickety-split to blazes out o' there, I should think," guessed Dido.

She added uneasily, "Hope they don't run up agin Cap'n Casket and the doc, though. Here's old man Breadno. All hunky-dory, Professor?"

"Ja. Is fastmakingness," he said sadly.

"Then we'd better be fast making tracks. Give the signal, Nate."

Nate gave two vigorous tugs on the rope, to indicate to Doctor Mayhew and the captain, at the other end, that the gun was now attached.

"Now, scarper, cullies—follow me!" Dido said. "We want to be well away from the rope after they fix it to old Rosie, or we're liable to have our feet scorched from under us. But keep low."

Crouching under their sheepskins, they hurried over the scribby ground as fast as they dared to the hollow where Dido had left the mule cart. Just as Nate was untying Mungo they were surprised by the report of a rocket, and its green light climbing up the sky illuminated their startled faces as they stared at one another.

"D'you suppose that's *them*?"

"Dunno, but whatever it is, we'd best hurry," Dido muttered. "Give Mungo a prod, Nate." They scrambled into the cart, and Mungo, who was not used to rockets, bolted away down the track towards Sankaty. They could see the lighthouse beam clear ahead of them.

"Shouldn't be far now," Dido said. "Wonder when old Rosie will start? They seem to be taking a pesky long time tying the rope to her tail. Oh, *Nate*—s'pose she acts up and won't have it, and skaddles off out o' reach?"

"Nonsense," he said more stoutly than he felt. "She'll do anything for Cap'n Casket—eat out o 'his hand."

Just before they reached the lighthouse they heard a choking, panting voice which called to them from the side of the road.

"Dido! Nate! Is that you? Oh, stop, please stop, it's Pen!"

"Why, Penny!" Dido jumped out of the cart and helped her in. "Are you all right, Pen? What's happened?"

"She—Aunt Trib—she's started for the forest—" gasped Penitence. "I can't—couldn't—stop her—" She had run so far and fast that her chest was heaving painfully; she pressed both hands against it but could not speak for several moments. "Climbed down to tell you—" she got out presently, "rocket—meant—fire—"

"Oh, poison," Dido said. "That rocket was their signal, you mean?"

Pen nodded, gulping in air. The others exchanged

glances of dismay at this confirmation of their fears. "So, any minute now—" said Dido. "Croopus, what in tarnation's Cap'n Casket—"

But as she spoke, her words were drowned by a vast, prolonged, ear-shattering bellow that seemed to make even the lighthouse tremble to its foundations. They heard the rope twang like a banjo string as the slack was suddenly drawn up. They heard a shrill, whistling hiss, like the whine of wind in rigging, as the rope flew over the uneven ground, cutting through sand, slicing off shrubs and sea grass. They heard a wild shout of warning from the dory, which came in sight round the lighthouse at this moment, Captain Casket and Doctor Mayhew rowing frantically for land. The tide was full, and the waves struck at the very foot of the cliff.

"Great candles!" cried Dido. "There she goes!"

As they strained their eyes seaward they had an instant's glimpse of the pink whale flashing across the lighthouse beam, half out of the water, arrow-straight and wild-eyed, with her flukes streaming behind her like pennants. Then she was gone, into the dark, heading north.

"Oh, *dear!*" said Pen. "I didn't think she'd like it! Supposing she don't forgive us and never comes back? Poor Papa will break his heart."

"Don't let's worry about *that* yet," said Dido. "He can go arter her when things has calmed down and feed her some cream buns or corn dodgers—the main thing is, now, will the rope hold? And where's Auntie Trib?"

Two minutes later her questions were to be dramatically answered.

With a low rumbling, which increased as it ap-

proached to a clamorous clattering din, the huge gun
rattled into sight, lurching over the rough ground on
its innumerable pairs of wheels, tipping and swaying
like a log in a torrent but, by a miracle, remaining
upright. "Look, *look!*" gasped Penitence, "there's
somebody on it!"

The light from the rising moon showed a wild figure clinging to the gun carriage—Aunt Tribulation,
astride the chassis, mad with rage, fiercely striking
match after match on the breech in a last, relentless
effort to fire the gun as it was dragged along. Not one
of the wet matches would light.

"She'll be over the cliff if she don't take care!"
Nate exclaimed.

Aunt Tribulation heard him. Observing for the
first time how near to the sea the gun had been
dragged in its headlong course, she abandoned the
matches and flung them from her with a curse. Shaking her fist at the party on the cart, screaming impre-
cations, she leapt with frantic agility up onto the
breech itself and ran, balancing like a tightrope
walker, along the barrel of the gun.

"She's got a knife!" cried Nate.

"She's going to cut the rope!"

"She'll never do it!"

"Yes, she will, by thunder!"

But even as she sawed furiously at the tough five-
inch Manila rope there came a last crazy lurch of the
gun—the muzzle dropped, the breech reared up into
the sky and remained poised for an instant on the
edge of the cliff—then the gun and its wild rider
plunged over and down, disappearing without a
sound into the white foam below.

CHAPTER ELEVEN

Mr. Jenkins returns. The civic banquet. The Thrush.
Another Aunt Tribulation. Goodby to the pink whale.

DIDO WOKE SUDDENLY and lay blinking in astonishment, not quite sure where she was. The sun was blazing in at the window, and somebody was perched on her chest, repeating over and over again in a patient voice, "Your Ladyship's bath is growing cold."

"Mr. *Jenkins!*" Dido exclaimed, coming to with a jerk. "Why, you funny old bird, how did you get here? Is the *Sarah Casket* in port, then?"

"Your Grace's wig needs a little powder," Mr. Jenkins replied. Dido jumped out of bed and began dressing. "Wake up, Penny!" she said, thumping the mounds of quilts on the other side of the bed. "Look who's here! Wake up, we've got visitors to cook breakfast for!"

But when they hurried downstairs they found that the visitors were already doing for themselves. Nate had been out milking, Professor Breadno wandered in with a hatful of eggs and a heron feather, while Doctor Mayhew was scientifically thumping away at a bowl of beaten-biscuit mixture.

"Look who's come!" Dido cried. Mr. Jenkins left her shoulder, where he had been sitting, and launched himself like a loving rocket at Nate's head, crying, "Oh, Your Excellency, I am afraid your sword has got caught in the carriage door."

Captain Casket's eyes lit up. He had been sitting in the rocker, looking a little sad and downcast, the only member of the party to do so; but now he brightened. "Why, Nate! Thy bird come back to thee! That must surely mean that the *Sarah Casket* has returned. We must set off for Nantucket town at once."

"Ay, that we must," Doctor Mayhew said. "My patients will be wondering if I've gone underground. And there is much to organize—a service of thanksgiving for having been saved from New York, and a civil banquet for our noble preservers—" He chucked Pen under the chin, pulled Dido's ear, and tweaked a lock of Nate's red hair. "Then we must send a warning about the *Dark Diamond* to the British Navy. Those miscreants must be caught."

"And I," Captain Casket said, "must find out the whereabouts of my sister Tribulation, in order that she may come and look after the children while I search for the pink whale."

Penitence suddenly burst into tears.

"Why, Penny!" Dido exclaimed in concern. "What's the matter, girl?"

"What ails thee, Daughter?"

"It's too unfair!" wept Penitence. "I tried so hard not to be afraid of Aunt Tribulation, and now it turns out she was the wrong one and I've got to start all over again."

"Never mind," Dido comforted. "The real one *couldn't* be any worse."

As soon as Nate had assured his mother of his safety, they all went in to Nantucket town together and made haste to the North Wharf, where the *Sarah Casket* was berthed. Great was the joy of the crew, particularly Uncle 'Lije, on seeing that Captain Casket and Nate were safe and not drowned, as had been thought.

"We reckoned as we'd make it a plum-pudding voyage, Cap'n," Mr. Pardon said, "and come back with only half our barrels full, for, to tell the truth, when we heard the pink 'un had been sighted off Nantucket I'd half a mind to wonder whether somehow you hadn't run aground here. I'm powerful glad we did come back. Hear there's been some everlastin' rum doin's in the old place since we left. Guess you'll be glad to put to sea again, Cap'n?"

"Yes, Mr. Pardon," Captain Casket said rather mournfully.

"He's pining for the pink 'un," Dido whispered to Nate, who nodded gloomily. However, they all cheered up during the civic banquet at the Grampus Inn, which was indeed a splendid affair. Professor Breadno, who had struck up a friendship with Doctor Mayhew, ate so many Nantucket Wonders that he was almost consoled for the loss of his gun, while Dido, Nate, and Penitence were toasted so often for their part in saving the island from disaster that they became quite bashful and retired out onto the balcony in order to recover their countenances. However, they had not been out there more than a few minutes when Dido came flying back to exclaim: "Doc Mayhew, do come and see. There's a British man-o'-war beyond the harbor bar and she's lowered a pinnace and the pinnace is a-coming into the harbor!"

"If she's looking for the plotters she's come to the wrong shop," Doctor Mayhew said. But he slung his mayoral chain round his neck again (he had taken it off for the easier consumption of scallops) and went out to greet the captain of the English sloop *Thrush*, who now came ashore, saluted, introduced himself as Captain Osbaldeston, and asked permission to make some inquiries about a gang of English criminals who were thought to have been lurking on Nantucket.

"You needn't bother, sir, you needn't bother!" Doctor Mayhew told him affably. "Mind you, so long as they'd left us alone, we'd 'a left *them* alone, and you could have saved your breath asking for them. But as we found 'em to be a nest of plaguy varmines we cleared them out ourselves. There's not one left on the island. Instead of losing time here you should be out chasing their schooner *Dark Diamond*—she's probably halfway to Land's End by now."

"Oh, no, she's not," Captain Osbaldeston corrected him. "She's lying in a hundred fathom of water in Massachusetts Bay."

"Eh?" exclaimed Doctor Mayhew, much startled by this information. "How did that happen, then? How did that come about?"

Captain Osbaldeston explained. He had just abandoned his fruitless search for *Dark Diamond* on the previous evening, he said, and was about to up anchor and make for home when, shortly after moonrise, he saw a schooner scudding along the Nantucket Coast under full press of sail. He thought it was his quarry.

"We were in the lee of the land at the time and she

didn't appear to see us; she was coming up fairly fast when, suddenly, the strangest accident befell her that ever I witnessed in all my life at sea."

"What happened?" Dido and Nate asked in one breath.

"Why, a thing that looked in the moonshine like a great pink whale came tearing along, half out of the water, dragging behind it what seemed to be a rope. It cut clean across the schooner's course, and when this rope struck the *Dark Diamond*, such was the speed of the whale's progress, if you will believe me, sir, that this rope sliced the schooner clean in two, before breaking with a twang like the Last Trump. The schooner sank in a matter of moments. It was an awesome sight, sir, it was indeed! Of course, we searched the waters roundabout, but we were unable to find any survivors."

"Then the world is well rid of a pack of trouble-makers," Doctor Mayhew observed cheerfully. "But won't you join our celebration, sir, since your task is at an end? Come in and drink a toast to our young friends here, who succeeded in getting rid of this nest of serpents for us."

Captain Osbaldeston observed that he would be very pleased to hear the whole story, so that he could include it in his report to the First Lord of the Admiralty. He came in and drank a great many glasses of ginger-jub while the tale was told. All agreed that the whale must have dragged the gun some distance along the sea bottom before the encounter with *Dark Diamond* parted the rope.

"So this young lady is a British citizen, is she?" Captain Osbaldeston presently inquired, looking at Dido. "Do you wish to be repatriated, madam?"

"To be whiched?"

"Would you like a passage back to England, my dear?"

Dido choked over a pickled tamarind. The temptation was almost irresistible. But she saw Pen's imploring eyes fixed on her and summoned the resolution to say, gruffly, "That's mighty civil of you, mister, and I thank you kindly, but I guess I'd better stick in Nantucket yet a while. I made a promise I'd stay with a friend till they was fixed up right and tight, which they ain't yet. So thanks, but not this time."

"In that case," Captain Osbaldeston said, "I'd best be on my way," and he bowed to the company and returned to his pinnace. Dido went out to watch it flit across the harbor and to take several deep breaths and rub a slight mistiness away from her eyes. As she stood on the balcony, slightly reluctant to go back to the gaiety of the banquet, she noticed the sails of another ship, a three-masted whaler, approaching Brant Point.

"Sail-o!" she called. "There's a-plenty traffic today."

The new ship, which presently revealed itself as the *Topsy Turvey*, came to anchor at length against the South Wharf, and everybody ran out to gaze at her in curiosity, for she was not a Nantucket vessel. The moment she was berthed, a stout lady who stood on deck had herself slung ashore in a barrel chair and came bustling along the wharf in a state of great excitement.

"Can anybody give me news of Captain Jabez Casket?" she asked. "Is he 'live or drownded? Why, there he *is*, his own self! Jabez! Brother Jabez! I declare, I never thought to see you more. I'd heard you was swallowed up by a pink whale!"

"Why, Sister Tribulation! I am amazed to see thee! Where has thee been?"

"And there's Mr. Pardon! And my old friend Enoch Mayhew—ho, ho, do you remember when you pushed me in the creek, you wicked old fellow!"

"Good gracious!" whispered Pen in Dido's ear. "Can *she* be Aunt Tribulation?"

The stout lady was cheerfully, even fashionably, dressed in pink-and-gray-striped sarcenet, with flounces, and a pink satin parasol, and cherries on her bonnet. She had black curls and gay black eyes, and her face was round and rosy and soft, like a pink frosted cake. She smelt strongly of lavender.

"Oh, don't call me Tribulation, please, Jabez—I have quite got out of *that* habit," she said laughing. "Sam always calls me 'Topsy.' Only fancy! I am married, Jabez! Here's my husband, coming ashore, Captain Sam Turvey. We got wed all of a sudden last fall, and I went off to sea with him. That was why I wrote my second letter saying that I should not, after all, be able to take care of Penitence in Nantucket. But, of course, when I heard you had been swallowed by the whale—"

"Second letter? But I had no second letter," he said, bewildered.

"Did you not? I sent it to Galapagos with Captain Bilger; I made sure you'd have had it by now. But where *is* Pen, then? How have you managed?"

She turned gaily round, exclaiming, "Now, which is my niece? Let me see if I can pick her out!"

"Here I am, Aunt Tribulation," Pen said shyly.

"'Topsy,' love, 'Topsy!' Never call me 'Aunt Tribulation!'" cried Aunt Topsy, enveloping Pen in a warm hug. "Yes, and I can see your mother in every

inch of you. But how you've grown, bless you! I'd not
have known you."

"I'd never have known *you*," Pen murmured.

"No, *that* you wouldn't," Dido muttered to herself,
amazed at the difference between Pen's three-year-old
memory of her aunt and this cheerful, pink-cheeked,
sweet-scented, bustling reality. Oh, dear, she thought,
why did this Auntie Trib have to go to sea? If only
she'd stayed on shore, everything would have been all
hunky-dory. Pen's taken a right fancy to her—anyone
can see that with half an eye.

It was true. Penitence was leaning happily in the
circle of Aunt Topsy's arm, her eyes shining like
stars.

". . . so, as I've decided that a life at sea doesn't
suit me," Aunt Topsy was saying, "I'm going to stay
right here in Nantucket and build me a house out at
'Sconset, for Sam to come back to between trips. And
you'll keep me company there, won't you, Penny,
when your papa's at sea?"

"Oh, yes!" Pen cried joyfully. "Oh, yes, Aunt
Topsy!"

"Oh, no!" groaned Dido involuntarily. "Oh, why
the blazes couldn't you have sailed in an hour ago instead of *now*? Then I coulda been snug aboard the
Thrush at this very minute, a-sailing back to London
River."

"Oh, Dido!" cried Pen remorsefully. "What a
shame! But you can stay with me and Aunt Topsy till
we find you another ship."

"It's all right—never mind." But Dido bit her lip.

Suddenly Captain Casket shook himself out of his
sad reverie.

"Nay!" he exclaimed, "but we'll up anchor with

the *Sarah Casket!* A Nantucket whaler can soon over-haul that lumbering English craft. We'll put thee aboard!"

"Oh!" cried Dido, "*could* you?"

Captain Casket was already rattling out orders: sails were shaken loose and the anchor was whisked up; half Nantucket town crowded on board to see Dido on her way.

The *Thrush* had a considerable start but was still in view, and the *Sarah Casket* rapidly began to gain on her as they crossed the Gulf of Maine. Then it could be seen that the *Thrush* was hauling her wind and bringing to; soon they saw the reason for this. Out of the northeast, arrowing through the ocean in a shower of spray like a broad piece of sunrise-colored ribbon came something that could only be the pink whale herself.

"It's Rosie!" Dido cried. "It's Rosie come back to look for the Cap'n!"

"Come back to see you off," said Nate.

"Come back to forgive us," said Pen softly.

Rosie frolicked round the *Sarah Casket* like a flying fish, and the bluejackets on board the *Thrush* crowded the rail to gaze in astonishment at this phe-nomenon.

Captain Casket hailed the *Thrush*.

"Hey, there! Cap'n Osbaldeston! Miss Twite would like to sail to England, after all."

"And welcome!" the *Thrush* replied; the captain's gig was sent across for Dido. She hugged everybody on the *Sarah Casket* goodby. Now that she was really leaving, she found herself sorry to say farewell; but just the same, she was happy—very, very happy—to be homeward bound at last.

"Come back soon, *dear* Dido!" said Pen. "Come and stay with me and Aunt Topsy next summer."

"Forvandel, blisschild," said Professor Breadno, who had accepted an invitation to stay with Doctor Mayhew on Nantucket and study snowy owls.

"So long!" said Nate.

"You'll always be welcome in Nantucket," said Doctor Mayhew. "You saved it from a fate far, far worse than death."

"Thee is a good child," said Captain Casket.

"Your Ladyship's carriage stops the way," said Mr. Jenkins.

Dido jumped down into the gig and was rowed across. When she reached the *Thrush* they piped her on board as if she had been the Queen herself, and the captain invited her to sit at his table. But she waited on deck, watching and waving until the *Sarah Casket*, escorted most joyfully by the pink whale, had started back to Nantucket and was out of sight.

When Dido returned next year to visit Pen, she found that Captain Casket had given up seafaring. Since the pink whale had returned, his only wish was to live on Nantucket and watch her every day as she sported and frolicked off its shores.

And, as whales and sea captains are both notoriously long-lived, it is possible that if you go to Nantucket today you may still have a sight of them.

Sweet whale of Nantucket, so pink and so round,
The pride of our island, the pearl of the Sound,
By Providence blest to our shores you were led,
Long, long may you gambol off Sankaty Head!